www.tredition.de

AF198286

For my Grandchildren

Christoph Werner

LIFTING THE IRON CURTAIN

Tales from a Bygone Country

Edited by Michael Leonard

www.tredition.de

German edition:
Mitgelaufen. Bertuch Verlag GmbH Weimar 2019

© Christoph Werner 2019

Editor: Michael Leonard
Layout: Helga Dreher

Published by tredition GmbH, Hamburg, Halenreie 40-44, 22359 Hamburg

ISBN
978-3-7497-8132-4 (Paperback)
978-3-7497-8133-1 (e-Book)

Table of Contents

FOREWORD

Much has been written about socialism but very little about what it was like to live as an ordinary citizen under socialism in East Germany. With the fall of the Berlin Wall now 30 years past, the realities of that time have begun to fade. Some have even become nostalgic, such as former Party functionaries and others who benefited from the communist rule. For the rest, however, I think it is important to bear witness to what it was really like to live in those times before the memories begin to vanish. What follows is by its nature far from complete because memory is not linear but impressionistic. Still, I hope the reader finds them of interest because they are the legacy of a lost socialist world.

Michael Leonard, who encouraged me to write these tales of a country bygone and then did his best to bring my English up to standard, has my lasting gratitude and praise for his efforts.

PRELUDE

May bug soar,
Father's at war,
In Pomerania Mother stays,
Pomerania's burnt away,
May bug soar.

Our maid used to sing this lullaby when she put us to bed. She was a *Pflichtjahrmädchen,* a "duty-year girl", a compulsory year of service for every girl under 25 years old that had been mandated by the Nazis in 1938. In order to prepare the girls for their future task as German mothers and at the same time to free every able-bodied man for service to the fatherland about 300,000 girls or young women per year had to work for twelve months on a farm, a small enterprise such as a restaurant, or often in a large family for a token wage of about 5 *Reichsmarks* per month, roughly the equivalent of 6 loaves of bread. We were four children and qualified as a large family. My mother even got the "Mother's Cross of Honor" for presenting the *Führer* with two daughters good for propagating the master race, and two sons useful as future soldiers to spread the master race over the globe.

Without this compulsory year a girl couldn't get an apprenticeship or a place in higher education. Sometimes those girls were used by the Nazis to spy on the families in which they worked. So, while my father was away in the war, my mother made sure that our maid was not in the house when she listened to the BBC, for which one could be sent to a concentration camp.

Our maid didn't of course realize how macabre this seemingly sweet song was, which was sung to the tune of

> *Sleep my child sleep.*
> *Your father tends the sheep.*
> *Your mother shakes the apple tree,*
> *As down a dream falls unto thee.*
> *Sleep my child, sleep.*

Some say the "May Bug Soar" song (German original: Maikäfer flieg) stems from the Thirty-Years' War (1618-1648), in which Pomerania suffered heavily. This war is still deeply ingrained in the German national memory and lives on in books, legends, anecdotes and songs. As soon as I could read, I devoured a shortened version of Grimmels-hausen's "Simplicissimus", a novel about the adventures of a boy in the Thirty-Years' War, and also stories and anecdotes about that time, of which my father had quite a number in his library. And of course, our father told us about the life of Paul Gerhardt, the writer or rather translator of "O Sacred Head Now Wounded" and the losses his family suffered during that war.

Our father had been sent to Romania, a lieutenant in an anti-aircraft unit, protecting the oil fields at Ploesti. At home we heard almost daily, towards the end of the war, the American and British bombers fly high over our village in the direction of the cities of Halle and Leipzig.

This filled the adults with both horror and relief, horror because many villagers including our family had friends or acquaintances in nearby Halle, and relief because they themselves were spared, at least for the time being. A large open-pit lignite mine and a briquette factory were situated near the village, and in order to destroy these facilities and thus damage the energy supply to the population and the weapon-producing factories in the region, they might have been a target for the bombers.

It must have been in the summer of 1944, when I was 5 years old, that I had been sent with my little basket on my back to the baker's to fetch bread. Suddenly the village's only siren on the local pub cum movie theater started howling, the streets were at once deserted and I found myself alone in the middle of a crossroads. A door opened and a man came running out and called to me in the local dialect: "Run home, boy!" This I did, startled and frightened, and before I even got to our street my mother came hurrying towards me, took hold of my hand and ran with me to the cellar, our air-raid shelter.

The American army arrived in the middle of April in our part of the country. They had, according to the Yalta Conference of February 1945, to withdraw their troops a few months later when the final border was established between the Western and Eastern zones of occupation. I and my classmates stood at the main street watching the American tanks driving through in pursuit of German tanks who had passed a short time before. At least this is what I remember. It seems quite unreal looking back on it now, but I can remember seeing the ragged uniforms of the German soldiers on their tanks and the clean and orderly battle dresses of the Americans following them.

I must have felt that something decisive had happened, because some time later I used an old rusty nail to scratch a swastika into a sandstone wall, obviously believing I had to do something for Germany. I recall looking around furtively while doing it, so I must have known that this was no longer acceptable.

When a bit older, about eight or nine, my classmates and I often talked about how "we" could have won the war had the miracle weapons the Führer had promised been produced in time.

In 1946 my father came home from an American prisoner of war camp in the Rhineland. He had been on leave in Germany and had thus escaped being seized by the Russians in Romania after the defeat.

They didn't get much to eat in the American camp, which he said he understood because the American army suddenly was in charge of more than a 100,000 prisoners in that camp alone, so when he was finally released he went first to his brother's estate in the American zone where he could once again eat his fill before returning home.

By then the Russians had arrived and my father as a former army officer had to report regularly to the military authority in the nearby *Kommandatura*.

He had taken up his old position as the village pastor and we lived in the very ancient rectory with a big garden, a backyard with a duck pond and a barn, which was rented out to a farmer. We also hosted evacuees from the former eastern parts of Germany now under Soviet and Polish administration. There were roughly 12 million of them, and for a while we had two families at the same time living in the attic.

Food at the time was very scarce. We kept chickens and rabbits, which helped, and in the summer and autumn, when raspberries and currants as well as tomatoes ripened, my brother and I were sent out into the garden with a slice of dry bread where we had our breakfast before setting off for school. The garden was big enough for my father to grow tobacco. I can still remember the smell from the attic, where he dried and then fermented the tobacco leaves from which he rolled his cigarettes or filled his pipe.

We used to cook sugar beets gathered from the fields in the autumn, cut into small pieces, in the laundry room to get sugar syrup. We boys had to take turns stirring the dark mass in the big copper pot with a huge wooden stirrer. Using sugar beets to this end was illegal, as the state needed the beets for the production of sugar, which was in short supply. My father, who never missed a chance of saying something derogatory about the new political system, maintained the sugar was needed to pay reparations due to the Soviet Union.

We also went out to the fields after the harvest to pick potatoes and grain such as barley, wheat, and rye left by the machines, that our mother turned into flour by means of the coffee grinder.

The farmers had it best (before they were collectivized), and when they celebrated weddings, baptisms and even funerals my father, after performing the ceremonies, was invited to take part in their meals and often brought home leftover cake for us. For a time, this happened so often that we became fed up with cake and couldn't eat any more, though on other days we went hungry.

I had a classmate, a farmer's son, whose lunch packet consisted of sandwiches thickly laid with butter, liverwurst or cheese, and I sometimes stood close to him during the breaks and watched him eat. From time to time he would offer me part of his lunch which I devoured hungrily, afterwards feeling ashamed.

My brother, one year older than I, once got severely caned by my father because he was so hungry that he entered the larder, which was off limits to us, and served himself from the jam pot and the bread. Later, when we were adults, my father told us how much he regretted that punishment.

On the whole our position as the children of the pastor was disadvantageous. Our father forbade us from sneaking into the apple and plum orchards as some people did—at harvest time they were guarded by the owner or tenant, who often spent the nights there in a hut with a fierce dog for assistance. But a few times we took part in the raids anyway, hid the apples or plums and devoured them in secrecy.

People also scavenged coal from the trains that had to slow down as they approached the suburbs of Halle. A number of my classmates climbed on the wagons and threw briquettes down which were then gathered and taken home. This was really a dangerous business because there were guards armed with clubs on every third or fourth wagon.

At that time the phrase "The Iron Curtain" began to be used. Although its popularity as a Cold War symbol is attributed to a speech Winston Churchill gave in March 1946 in Fulton, Missouri, the German Minister of Popular Enlightenment and Propaganda, Joseph Goebbels, had already used the term in reference to the Soviet Union in 1943.

For a time, at least until the construction of the Wall in 1961, the border between East and West Germany was more symbolic than an actual fortified frontier. There was in fact no Iron Curtain between the two Germanys, and if you knew your way about you were able to cross "the green border" without much danger. It was even easier in Berlin, where you simply got onto the municipal railway in East Berlin and alighted in West Berlin.

One day around 1950 my father decided I was to spend my summer holidays at his brother's in West Germany. He contacted a *frater-in-Christo,* a Lutheran minister who had his parish near the border in the Harz Mountains, and he helped us find a footpath through fields and woods that landed us in West Germany.

This was my first outing to the free world. When my father and I had walked to the nearest railway station in the West, we felt hungry and entered a butcher's shop to get a roll with minced meat. I remember how the woman behind the counter looked at what she thought must be a starved child from the East. She gave us two bread rolls with sausage, which tasted delicious. When re-crossing the border on our way home, we were caught by a border guard and my father was fined a sum of money.

In 1949, the founding year of the German Democratic Republic (East Germany), we moved from the village to a suburb of Halle. It was the time of the Marshall Plan, which had helped create the *Wirtschaftswunder* in West Germany. The East German Government, under the orders of Stalin, refused all assistance from the imperialist West. I remember a poster with the slogan "We do not need a Marshall Plan; we crank up the economy ourselves".

At the time, there was also a growing hostility to the *Junge Gemeinde,* a kind of congregation of the young within a protestant parish. This was not an organization in its own right, but a special form of activity within the parish embracing young Christians. The supreme body of the Party, the Politburo, passed a "Plan for the Exposure of the Young Christians as a Camouflage Organization for Warmongering, Sabotage and Espionage directed by West German and American Imperialist Agents". Those who refused to leave the Young Christians were thrown out of secondary schools and universities.

Though I was the son of a pastor and active in the Young Christians, they couldn't expel me from the school since it was the primary school, which was mandatory for everybody to their fourteenth year. I had little hope however of being accepted to high school. But luckily, our examination in *Gegenwartskunde,* a kind of social studies, actually a subject of purely political indoctrination, was due to be held on

17 June, but hurriedly cancelled because of the June 1953 uprising.

People obviously believed in an imminent toppling of the communists, so some teachers said they would give me good grades to help me continue my education at high school.

This belief was not absolutely unfounded, given Soviet strong man Berija's plans for the future of East Germany. They were not common knowledge, but that something was going on behind the scene and particularly behind the backs of the East German communist party was whispered about. In the wake of the June uprising, Beria was suspected of being willing to trade the reunification of Germany and the end of the Cold War for massive aid from the United States, as had been received by the West after World War II. Now the East German uprising convinced the other Soviet leaders that Beria's policies were dangerous and destabilizing to Soviet power. Within days of the events in East Germany Party Secretary Khrushchev organized a Party coup against Beria. On June 26, 1953, that is ten days after the beginning of the revolt in Berlin, Beria was arrested, tried and executed with his closest allies in December 1953.

The *SED* (East German Communist Party) headed by First Secretary Walter Ulbricht, whose very existence had been in jeopardy during the uprising, was again securely in control.

But of course, I wasn't aware of any of those things on 17 June, incidentally a Wednesday. I got on my bicycle and went to the center of Halle, where about 60,000 people had gathered on the Market Place in front of the town hall, which was cordoned off by Soviet soldiers, supported by a number of tanks, which from time to time moved forward a few meters to push people back. A man said to me to be careful with my bicycle because if I should fall in the crowd, I couldn't get away quickly enough to escape the tracks of the tanks.

Everybody rejoiced, communist banners and pictures of the so-called representatives of the working class were torn down, functionaries when recognized abused, sometimes beaten up, and a general belief that everything would basically change for the better took hold of the crowd. I watched a truck breaking the doors of the remand prison, and the prisoners set free, including those who were investigated for their involvement in Nazi crimes before 1945.

The East German communist party and government turned to the Soviet army for help, which together with the People's Police crushed the uprising, during which many people lost their lives or received prison sentences.

Despite the communists' promises to change the course of its policies and make life better and more democratic, it soon turned out that these promises were just a means to keep people calm. But at least I could continue my education and eventually go on to the university.

1 FREEDOM OF EXPRESSION

My bell was ringing as if a very determined thumb was pressing the button. The November day was dark. A slight cold rain fell, with gusts of wind pushing against the old window-panes of my student digs, making them rattle. I had just settled down in my clammy study to work on my examination paper about Graham Greene's latest book, *A Burnt-Out Case*, and was losing myself in the characters of Querry, Dr. Colin and Rycker. My brother in West Germany had promised to send me as much secondary literature on Greene as he could lay his hands on. He had smuggled *A Burnt-Out Case* into the German Democratic Republic when he had last visited me. The frontier was still sort of open, the erection of the Berlin Wall one year ahead of us.

Since I was impatiently waiting for the mail service to deliver the promised books and journals, I jumped up and ran to the door to get the parcel from the postman. But alas, it was not the postman who had rung. Instead, two tall gentlemen in the uniforms of customs officers were looming above me and asking, could they come in? I was so surprised that it didn't occur to me to inquire what they wanted. And anyway, being a well-trained GDR citizen and a German at that, I respected uniforms as a matter of course.

When they had settled down on my bed and my only spare chair, one of them, obviously the ranking officer, started to inform me that a parcel with books and journals from Hanover (in West Germany) had been impounded by their customs comrades, because it contained printed material from the class enemy. I ventured to answer that I was expecting books by and about the British author Graham Greene, who was well-known for his critical attitude toward Western imperialism and who particularly disliked the Americans, as could be seen from his book *The Quiet American*. And, moreover, this book had been favorably reviewed in the *Organ of the Central Committee of the Socialist Unity Party, SED, Neues Deutschland*. I soon suspected the two comrades to be officers from the district branch of the Ministry of State Security (or *Stasi*), so to put them in a good mood I used the full title of the *Neues Deutschland* newspaper and let it be known by my remark and the tone in which it was voiced that I was an avid and faithful reader of the Party's most important instrument of popular enlightenment and propaganda.

But they insisted that the propaganda of the class enemy came disguised in many forms, so that under the cover of a certain anti-Americanism an author like Greene could easily get into the minds of unsuspecting and, particularly, young people. Had he not maintained that society can only be changed by first making the individual happy? Now I was flabbergasted. Educated *Stasi*-people, who even knew about Graham Greene? And was it not, the other visitor chimed in, the socialist revolution, the fundamental changes in our country, that was the precondition for making the individual happy? And not, as my author wanted to make us believe, the other way around? And what about the representation of our Soviet friends in *The Third Man*?

I asked, well, what about it? "There you are," said the man, "you didn't even notice in what a disparaging way the Soviet military policeman in the Vienna International Patrol is described?" He took a slip of paper from his jacket pocket and read from it: "When they arrested Anna in the early hours of the morning, she was still in bed. The Russian, not giving Anna an opportunity of letting him in, put his shoulder to the door and tore out the bolt. They got in and told Anna to get dressed. The writer goes on to say that the Russian watched Anna dressing while the Englishman left the room. The Frenchman watched the reflection of the girl dressing in the mirror of the wardrobe. The American, of course, would never leave a girl unprotected with a Russian soldier and so stayed in the room but with his back chivalrously turned."

He looked up from his notes and said, in a harsh voice that I ought to be able to see (if I wanted to, that is) that the Soviet soldier, a soldier of the glorious Red Army, which had borne the main burden of the fight against the Nazis, was being shown here as inferior, and as prone to raping women.

And that's why we can't allow such literature in our country, he added.

We know, the ranking officer said, that you have in your possession a number of books by Greene, and we tolerate it, because you are a student of English literature. But if you need reviews, interpretations, *etc.*, you are asked to turn to GDR or Soviet sources.

Later I learned that the institute where I was studying English had been paid an unannounced visit by two men who wanted to speak to my professor. The secretary, with whom I was on very good terms, told me that she had heard my name through the closed door to the professorial study. So they had obviously been academically briefed by the professor, who, by the way, sat in the East German Parliament representing a constituency in the district of Halle, my university town.

One may now wonder why the Ministry of Truth, excuse me, the Ministry of State Security, bothered so much with a simple and well-meaning student. There are, I believe, a number of reasons, most of which I only became aware of later, when I read my *Stasi* files after the fall of the Berlin Wall.

First of all, my studies of English and German were intended to produce a teacher for the Extended Secondary School, or *Gymnasium* (high school) as it's called today. And well-qualified English teachers were rare, the older generation from before the war having been pensioned off for the most part, and Nazi teachers removed after 1945. And there were not enough applicants for teacher training. So they tried to keep me on board and at the same time make me ideologically acceptable. Also, the border to West Germany was still open at that time and one could easily leave the country via Berlin. In July 1961 alone, the month before the building of the Wall, 30,000 people managed to leave East Germany.

Secondly, my father was a Lutheran minister, and at the time I am referring to the state had just begun to ease up on the church, and they possibly feared that he might cause trouble via the church authorities.

Thirdly, they wanted to keep an eye on me—as I learned from my files much later—because I had once made fun of the gymnastics that we had to do during lecture breaks, comparing that somewhat alien activity to the physical jerks so heartbreakingly described by George Orwell in *1984*. That book had also been spirited across the border from West Germany by my brother. The "Unofficial *Stasi* Informant" (*Inoffizieller Mitarbeiter*, or IM) in my student group had categorised my remarks as hostile-negative. (But that, as I said, I only learnt from my files.) Also, I was at that time not a member of the communist youth organization *FDJ* (all of my fellow-students were) and therefore required special attention.

By the way, the physical jerks were discontinued not much later, which I regretted to some extent as watching the girls jumping up and down had had a positive effect on my mood.

The fourth reason which I think might have contributed to the Sword and Shield of the Party (as the *Stasi* liked to see themselves) keeping tabs on me was a correspondence I had with a friend in Rostock on the Baltic coast. He had been studying medicine there and had taken part in an illegal leaflet campaign, in which the bigoted information policy of the communists was criticized. My friend was thrown out of the university and fled to West Germany via the "green frontier", thereby risking his freedom. The secret police undertook a search of his flat, found my letters, in which I had referred to Party functionaries unflatteringly as "bonzes", and notified the district attorney of Rostock, who then ordered a search of my digs.

Now that had been interesting. Two men on a motorcycle—they hadn't even thought me important enough to justify the use of a car—stopped in front of the old house and asked for admission. They then produced a warrant from the district attorney and began a search of my study. They took away some folders with typed sheets and notes connected with my examination paper, and copies of my letters to my friend in Rostock.

Nothing official came of the house search except that my then girlfriend, who shared the flat with me and hadn't been present during this procedure, threw her hands up and said that, for heaven's sake, she hadn't dusted the (sparse) furniture that day, and what would the men now think of her? Her relationship to the state was a very trusting one, and I later heard that she had joined the *SED*.

With regard to trying to get printed material, books, newspapers and journals from West Germany or other capitalist countries, I read much later about the following incident.

Hermann Kant, president from 1978 to 1990 of the East German Writers' Union, who was a *Stasi* informant with the code-name "Martin", complained to his *Stasi* controller about the ignorance of the GDR customs administration. The Dutch Minister for Trade had sent a copy of the novel *Billiards at Half-Past Nine* by Heinrich Böll (who later won the Nobel prize for literature) to a well-known political figure in the GDR. The book was confiscated and a notification sent to both the sender and the addressee that the book was of an anti-democratic character and could therefore not be allowed in.

All this despite the fact that an East German publishing house planned to publish the book the following year in the GDR! Imagine the use the Minister in the Netherlands will make of this in the press. Kant's controller promised he would inform his superiors of the need to educate and enlighten their otherwise-so-dedicated warriors.

It may well be that this fresh approach had already borne fruit in my case, and that they had taken the trouble to inform themselves about the matter in question. Of course, this would not go as far as to let all kinds of books through, but at least they had tried to convince the person for whom the book was intended, which was of course a futile endeavor.

Anyway, I succeeded in finishing my paper on Greene, though not without my professor proposing some major alterations. To her mind there was too much talk of damnation, redemption, hell, and so on, too much of the murky territory of shifting boundaries typically inhabited by Greene's characters, in short, too much Greeneland. She suggested that I insert a sizable amount of Marxist terminology—ideological highlights, she called them— which I duly did. So additional text was added about socialism brightening the horizon, which Greene not so much made explicit but allowed the reader to sense in the subtext, and so on. She also hinted that she would prefer a conclusion along the lines that Greene (at least for a time) had been a comrade-in-arms of the socialist countries in their fight against Western colonialism. This didn't contribute much to a better understanding of Greene, but it did get me a good mark.

Luckily the paper went astray when the institute moved to other premises, so I didn't feel ashamed about it for too long afterwards. And there was always the consolation that to further their careers most people worked like that.

As for reading Western journals, I remember what a professor of Political Economy once told me "between you and me and the lamp-post". Since his main area of work at the university was the economics of capitalism, from time to time he needed Western sources for his work—in this case it was the West German *Spiegel* magazine. They had a so-called poison cabinet at their institute where such documents were held under lock and key, and were only accessible to the director and the Party secretary. When the professor needed a certain article, the Party secretary would fetch the journal, open it at the specified place and let the scholar read it, carefully ensuring that he didn't befoul his socialist consciousness by wandering off onto other pages.

After having finished my studies I worked for two years—that was mandatory—as a school teacher. Very soon I got into trouble with the school inspector, who sat in on one of the weekly meetings of the staff. This was in the year 1962, when the Berlin Wall and the 1400 km fortified frontier had not been in place for long.

The healthy and useful separation from West Germany was still a much-discussed topic, and was also a subject in lessons. As the English master I was allowed to read the British communist paper the *Daily Worker* (some years later renamed the *Morning Star*) and to use it for teaching purposes in my classes. Now at that time (and virtually from the start) the *Daily Worker* had failed to use the designation "anti-fascist barrier" preferred by the GDR authorities and particularly recommended for schools, and would refer to the Wall as—"the Wall". Now, fool and eager beaver that I was, I quoted the *Daily Worker*'s arguments, which praised the Wall as an effective means of stabilizing the East German economy, and I called the Wall the Wall, as I thought that I should use authentic English.

Just a few days before that I had talked in another of my lessons about English nursery rhymes, citing among them *Humpty Dumpty sat on a wall, Humpty Dumpty had a great fall; all the king's horses and all the king's men couldn't put Humpty together again.* The son of the school inspector, who had difficulty following my enlightened teaching and generally got bad marks, in this case successfully managed to learn the nursery rhyme by heart (as I had told the class to do) and he quoted it to his father.

In the staff meeting I was then severely called to order by the inspector. What had come into my mind to allow, willingly or not, a comparison between our anti-fascist bulwark (that was the word he used, having obviously consulted a dictionary for the word *Bollwerk*) and a capitalist nursery rhyme, thus belittling the historic fortification of our frontier in Berlin? I remained mute and looked so contrite that the headmaster intervened, referring to my youth and inexperience as a teacher, and promising to look after me better in the future. So I was spared the procedure known as "extensive self-criticism" (which was regarded as the first step to betterment).

I was aware of the fate of the East German author Erich Loest, who at that same time was spending a seven-year-sentence in Bautzen II, a *Stasi* penitentiary known for its particularly strict discipline. The rogue writer had taken part in discussions on the need for de-Stalinization in the GDR and, even worse, pleaded for the removal of Walter Ulbricht from his post as the First Secretary of the Central Committee of the Socialist Unity Party (*SED*). He was consequently brought to trial and, with others, convicted of having taken part in a "counter-revolutionary grouping". The most eager of the debaters had actually been an informant. While I was sitting in the staff meeting, I had of course remembered the article in the *Neues Deutschland* newspaper on Christmas Eve, 1958, informing its readers, us students included, that Loest and others had formed a subversive group and been punished accordingly. That didn't really encourage political criticism of any kind, and therefore I was glad to get away with my Humpty Dumpty/Wall pun.

It is interesting how highly the communists regarded the influence of literature on the minds of their people—and how much they overrated it. I suspect that they never lost sight of Stalin's words that "writers are engineers of the human soul". They obviously still believed that, just as an engineer can put a well-functioning machine together, so a writer could make the human soul function in a predetermined and desired way.

Erich Loest, incidentally, found two of his own books in the prison libraries: a collection of love stories, in the remand prison of the city of Halle, popularly known as "The Red Ox", and one of his novels, in the Bautzen II penitentiary. The *Stasi* had clearly not been thorough enough in cleansing these libraries, and had done a poor job of making Loest an unperson. In his autobiography, the writer said that this took them another year. Later, when I was a lecturer in the English department of a technical college, I had another stroke of good fortune in connection with the affair of the pugnacious poet, writer and singer Wolf Biermann. He had angered the GDR authorities too much and was duly stripped of his GDR citizenship in 1976. This happened while he was on an officially authorized tour in West Germany, and it provoked protests from prominent GDR writers and intellectuals.

Many persons and institutions were now approached by the authorities to sign resolutions supporting Wolf Biermann's expulsion, even though his name was little-known among us ordinary folk. I for one had never heard of him before I read his name in *Neues Deutschland*. But that did not matter, we were told by the Party secretary of our department, we should simply trust the Party and sign the resolution to be published in *Neues Deutschland*. It was my luck that I fell ill and had to stay at home for a few days, so the resolution went ahead and was printed without my name being on it. I was thus spared a moral decision in which I am not sure how I would have responded.

To be fair, I have to add the following. Before the German Democratic Republic collapsed in 1989-1990, I left the country by means of an exit permit, for which I and my family had been waiting for three years (and for which we were punished by losing our work). In my new job at a provincial university in West Germany I also had the choice occasionally of speaking up or keeping my mouth shut in order not to risk losing my temporary employment or rather the prolongation of my contract. This reveals what I suspect is one of the commonest traits of human character, or at least of *my* character, which can be fittingly summed up in the words of Bertolt Brecht: First the grub, *then* the morals.

There was a very close relationship between the print media (indeed, *all* media in East Germany) and the Party. A few years after Erich Honecker, with the help of Leonid Brezhnev, had become the supreme leader of the country, having forced his predecessor Walter Ulbricht to step aside I met a young man on the staircase in front of our flat. He was my neighbor in the newly-built city of Halle-Neustadt, about 20-years-old, and working in the printing shop of the district of Halle *SED* newspaper *Freiheit* (meaning "liberty"). He was very excited and told me that he had to rush to his place of work, as something very grave had happened there.

Just as the first copies of the newspaper were about to be sent out to the subscribers and kiosks that day, an alert colleague had by chance held the front page against the morning sun outside the shop and discovered a frightful coincidence. A photo of Erich Honecker showed a black bar across his forehead!

How had this come about? The black bar shone through from another photo on the back of the front page, and was actually scaffolding which was still in place around a new building in Halle-Neustadt, much praised for its size and its low-rent flats. A dark-colored, wooden board of this scaffolding shone through the paper, giving the General

Secretary of the Central Committee of the Socialist Unity Party a *Brett vorm Kopf* (or "board across his head"), which is a not very nice way of saying that someone is a blockhead.

Newspaper readers, the young man admitted, do not usually hold newspapers against the sun when reading them, but what if it should happen? He had therefore been called, on his day off, to hurry to his place of work to help pulp the 50,000-odd copies already printed. And so he rushed off, though not without telling me of the damage this mistake could have done had the class enemy got wind of it!

The intimate relationship between the Party and the media, in this case *Neues Deutschland*, could have far-reaching and unexpected consequences. One day, I believe it was in the early 1980s, the paper announced in a small article that the monthly payments for old-age pensioners, which were notoriously low, were to be increased, I don't remember by what percentage.

Now at that time I had an acquaintance who had an acquaintance who knew somebody in the GDR government. And thus, I learned that neither the government nor the Party had planned to increase the pensions, nor could the country afford this increase economically. But since the newspaper was the Organ of the Central Committee of the Party and thus could never err, and also since people had long been waiting for such an increase, the pensions were indeed grudgingly raised by a modest amount, thus adding to the national debt. The editor responsible for this fake but rectified news was said to have been banished to the Letters to the Editor department, an outcome that could have been much worse. As if to make amends, the newspaper in its edition of March 12th, 1984, contained no fewer than 43 (!) photos of General Secretary Erich Honecker visiting the Leipzig Trade Fair.

A reporter on Radio DDR kept his job, however, even though he mistakenly thought he could crack a joke by saying in the morning radio program: "As there are no bananas to be had at the moment, cheer up and eat an extra egg."

Why people in East Germany were so stubbornly reluctant to believe in the cause of socialism may have been because they got ninety percent of their direct information from West German radio and TV.

The West German magazine *Tempo* came up with the following prank: On March 19th, 1988, a number of people in East Berlin and the German Democratic Republic found in their mailboxes or on their doorsteps as well as in railway stations, phone booths and other public places copies of *Neues Deutschland* that were actually complete fakes. The Hamburg magazine had produced 6,000 copies of the newspaper that looked exactly like the real thing, and contained the most outrageous news.

For example, that *glasnost* ("transparency"), Gorbachev's new political course in the Soviet Union, was to be introduced in the GDR, that 5,000 political prisoners had been set free, that dissidents who had fled East Germany were asked to return and promised a hearty welcome, and that the most stubborn and obtuse members of the Political Bureau, the real center of power in the country, had been fired. And, to crown it all: that the Ministry of State Security had been abolished.

From now on people would be able to buy *Playboy* magazine (sporting the German title *Spielmann,* literally "Playman"), and travel agencies would offer flights to Los Angeles, Rome and Madrid, taking off from either Schönefeld (in East Berlin) or Tegel (in West Berlin), whichever the passengers preferred.

Neues Deutschland, the real one, waited almost ten days before it published a lame denial, saying that "a primitive fake of *Neues Deutschland,* produced in West Germany, had been disseminated", and that this would not help improve relations between the two countries. Of course, nothing was said about the contents of the fake publication.

This was no doubt one of the few times when people read the newspaper with any real interest. Nothing is known about the number of people in the GDR who were taken in by the deception. Probably not very many, as the announced measures and news items sounded too good to be believable. One and a half years later, though, every promise had come true.

It is one of the great ironies of recent history that the *SED* in October/November 1989, after they had got rid of Erich Honecker and replaced him with Egon Krenz as the new General Secretary, Chairman of the National Defense Council and Chairman of the State Council, initiated their own downfall.

Thousands of demonstrators in the streets of Berlin and other major cities in East Germany, notably Leipzig, had finally lost their fear. They forced the Party and the government (which were virtually identical) to start those very reforms that had been so mischievously reported in the fake edition of *Neues Deutschland*. But it was too late. Frantically shoring up their Stalinist regime, they had simply clung to power for too long.

I was in West Germany at the time, and I watched the famous press conference of Günter Schabowski on TV. Ever since then I have been very fond of the German word *unverzüglich*. To an English native speaker this word, with its eerie umlaut (ü), may look and sound sinister but to me it has a very sweet ring to it. In fact, the word is rather old-fashioned and literary, and tends not to be used much in everyday German. But Günter Schabowski, member of the Political Bureau, being an educated man, did indeed use it.

When Schabowski was asked, in the press conference on November 9th, 1989, when the new travel regulations announced by the government were actually to come into force, he was caught off-balance. He fumbled with his papers, stuttered, and finally said that people were free to travel to the West *unverzüglich*, *i.e.*, right away, immediately. He did this forgetting or overlooking the fact that his boss Egon Krenz had fixed an embargo on that item until 4 o'clock the following morning.

As a consequence, the frontier guards, first at the check points in Berlin and later along the entire western frontier of the GDR, were taken by surprise, and virtually overwhelmed by the crowds eager to take advantage of the new freedom. Left helpless, and in the absence of orders from their superior officers, the guards opened the barriers and let the people through. So, when the SED at long last moved towards replacing freedom of suppression with freedom of expression —of which the Schabowski press conference was a sure indication —they inadvertently brought their own regime crashing to the ground.

2 HOW I HELPED COLLECTIVIZE EAST GERMAN AGRICULTURE

The study of Old and Middle English in my first years at Halle University was certainly fascinating, though the other students and I were of two minds about it. True, I can still recite the beginning of King Alfred's Preface to the translation of Gregory's Pastoral Care: Ælfred kyning hateð gretan Wærferð biscep his wordum luflice & freondlice; & ðe cyðan hate ðæt me com swiðe oft on gemynd, hwelce wiotan iu wæron giond Angelcynn, ægðer ge godcundra hada ge woruldcundra ... (King Alfred greets bishop Wærferth lovingly with his words and friendship; and I let it be known to thee that it has very often come into my mind, what wise men there formerly were throughout England, both of sacred and secular orders ...)

Though still in the first third of our studies we were already advanced thinkers enough to realize that it would have been more important as future teachers of English to spend our time learning a slightly more modern variant of this beautiful language. But the curriculum and our professor, God bless his soul because he taught us a tolerable English pronunciation in his phonetic exercises, wanted it so. Just as we were approaching the lament of King Alfred about the lack of wise men on this side of the Humber, the government, or was it the Party, which in most cases were one and the same, called on us for help.

What had happened? The stubborn farmers or at least quite a number of them, though they were living in the first "workers' and peasants' state on German soil", refused to join the newly founded agricultural cooperatives. To say the truth, they did not really object openly, but cleverly signed the declaration of entry into the collective in order to escape the pressure exerted on them, and then did nothing else. They went on working their fields and farmsteads as before, privately, much to the chagrin of the ailing collectives, which to survive and even to grow urgently needed new members with their machines, cattle, draught horses, labor force, sheds and fields.

It was one of the great aims of the ascendant socialist state to transform the agricultural sector in the same way they had transformed the industrial sector. That meant getting rid of the traditional organizations and elite members of the rural society, which included the so-called wealthy farmers and large-scale landowners (those who owned more than 100 hectares of land), the Raiffeisen cooperatives (Raiffeisen was a social reformer from the middle of the 19th century and conceived of the idea of cooperative self-help), the credit unions, the private agricultural trade and the plant and breeder's associations. They were all regarded as hostile to progress and possible bases for the reactionary forces opposed to the introduction of socialism. This followed the Soviet example of forced collectivization under Stalin, though in the Soviet Union it entailed millions of dead.

So one day in 1960, just before the beginning of our lectures, a Free German Youth (the communist youth organization) meeting was called and we were told of an important political undertaking, in which we had the honor and of course the damn duty of participating, alongside other politically reliable citizens drawn from a number of urban and rural institutions including staff from universities and polytechnics, officials from State Owned Farms as well as functionaries from all political parties and mass organizations. So you could say we were in good company.

An instructor from the University Party Group explained to us that we were needed in the countryside to convince farmers of the necessity of joining the *LPG*s not just in words or by their signatures, but indeed, by placing their fields and machines etc. under the authority of the cooperative. Nominally, they would remain in possession of their land, but from then on as members of a collective or association.

Wilfried Bauermann, who always had a question or a doubt, but mostly got away with it because he managed to clad it in Party speak, said that he didn't believe that we students, mostly city people and as such "ignorant townies" could convince farmers, who were for a large part *Neubauern*, New Farmers, beneficiaries of the postwar land reforms and as such particularly proud of their new possession, of the advantages of joining the collective. But then Dagmar Ziegener piped up asking Wilfried if he doubted the wisdom of the Party, which had after all decided that we students were up to the task. Dagmar had obviously been instructed beforehand by the faculty Party group to break any resistance to the brilliant plan. So, we formed what was called *Festigungsbrigaden*. It is difficult to find an English equivalent for this, as it was a word coined for the occasion and never used again. It did not find its way into the German dictionaries. Perhaps an explanatory translation would serve: A group formed temporarily to help convince the farmers to fully join the cooperatives. Maybe one could call it an agitation brigade. So Wilfried Bauermann, Dagmar and myself formed a *Festigungsbrigade.*

This was of course folly. We ignorant young people, accustomed to town life were to go among the harassed farmers (so harassed that many of them had taken part in the GDR-wide uprising on June 17, 1953) and talk them into something they most of them had hated from the beginning. As for myself, I had spent my childhood up to my tenth year in a farming village and there had become acquainted with the life and work of the farmers. I had watched horses being shoed by the farrier, had even seen steam plows (the last of their kind) working the fields and had sat on a horse that was drawing a machine that turned over the hay after cutting. My greatest experience was watching a stallion covering a mare, but when I asked the farmer what was the good of that huge animal jumping upon the mare, I didn't get a satisfying answer. Anyway, life in a village was not alien to me and I was in fact looking forward to a week on a farm, and, to be honest, a week near pretty Dagmar, though we didn't share the same *weltanschauung.* (As it turned out, Wilfried outstripped me in that respect and, as he later boasted to me, had quite an agreeable roll in the hay with her. He said it gave him quite a kick imagining he was raping the Party). The other girls in our student group were different. They were most of them nice to look at, but too vulnerable for a callous approach and not at all familiar with life in the country nor with rolls in the hay. I will come to that later.

Our brigade traveled by train from Halle to Karl-Marx-Stadt in Saxony, today Chemnitz again (I wonder what Karl would have said had he seen the things that were visited upon the people), and there distributed among various places in the district. Ours went first to Reichenbach *im Vogtland*, a historic town from the 13th century in the Vogtlandkreis county of Saxony.

From there we were taken by car to our assigned village of Waldhausen (I am using fictitious names as I do not know if the persons I met would agree to having their true identities revealed). I was delivered to Albin Schröter, one of the New Farmers, who appeared to be a youngish man of about thirty with a friendly wife and a ten-year-old son. I still don't know how the *SED* (communist) functionaries from Reichenbach Regional Administration, Department for Agriculture, had cajoled this farmer to take in a student, and not just accommodate and feed him, but allow him to pester him with political talk. But this is what he did. Albin, as one of the administration people had told me, had the nickname "Albin the Last", a reference to a propaganda film comedy produced by the state titled just so because he had been the last in the village to sign his entry into the cooperative, which meant he was a hard nut to crack. And I was to be the nutcracker! Unbelievable, but true.

Frau Schröter gave me a bedroom under the roof of the farmhouse with a huge feather eiderdown and a chamber pot, the privy being at the dung heap in the yard. Then she called me down to have supper with them in a very big low-ceilinged kitchen heated by a large rustic cast-iron stove.

As a student I was rather thin, almost undernourished, and observed with mouth-watering anticipation the various kinds of sausages and spreads such as blutwurst, liverwurst, mettwurst, bacon and butter. There were freshly-baked bread and boiled eggs, and milk for the son and the wife. Albin and I had beer. It was very awkward at the beginning, since nobody around the table knew what to talk about. Then I decided it was for me to begin. I told them why the powers had sent us students here, that I had no idea how to go about my assignment, that I had spent my childhood in a village and would like to work with the farmer and maybe learn something of his problems. Their faces cleared, and we heartily fell to eating. The boy, Kilian, began to talk about school and how some of his classmates had taunted him about his father's reluctance to fully join the collective. His father suggested that this had probably been instigated by one of the teachers.

After finishing supper, Kilian was sent to bed, Frau Schröter, first name Ingrid, busied herself with the washing up, and Albin offered me a cigarillo. We lit up, drank from our mugs and looked at one another for a while without saying anything.

Obviously, Albin was considering how far he could trust me. Then he gave himself a push and told me about his difficulties and his refusal to join the collective, or rather his indecision. He more or less implied that there were no secrets in his talk as he had used such arguments in his discussions with the *LPG* adherents, of course minus some abusive words.

It appeared that his father and grandfather had been farmhands on a nearby manor, which due to its size of over 100 hectares fell under the land reform of 1945-46. His father on his return from an American POW camp was given a New Farmstead, which had been an outlying estate or grange of the old manor and as such equipped with farmhouse, barn and stables.

Albin was born in 1930 and was lucky in that the lady of the manor, who was later arrested with her family by the communist authorities and transported to the isle of Rügen, from where they fled to the West, had taken an interest in him and let him make use of their library in the mansion, where he read all the old Germanic heroic legends, Grimm's tales but also Karl May's Red Indian books. Even as a boy of ten he had started the habit of looking up things he did not understand in the lady's "Meyer's Great Encyclopedia" (*Meyers Großes Konversationslexikon*).

His father had obviously had good connections with the local land reform enforcers, because it was a great advantage to have gotten this estate, which even had a still functioning old threshing machine driven by an even older one-cylinder external diesel engine, 1920s vintage. Originally a Lanz-Bulldog two-stroke hot-bulb tractor had been part of the machinery, but had to be handed over to the *LPG*.

Having got so far, Albin said that he would now like to call it a day and go to bed. If I liked I could get up with him at 5 the next morning, have breakfast, feed the cows and horses and start the potato crop on the field behind the barn. Ingrid, his wife, Albin said, would be up earlier, at four, feed the chicken and pigs, milk the cows and prepare breakfast for the family. Little Kilian had it best, school starting at 8, so he would get up at 7.

Albin had two horses, both of which were about 10 years old and the offspring of a mare that had served in the war and got out unharmed. Did you know, Albin asked me, that the greater part of the means of transport of the *Wehrmacht* were horses? That is what his father had told him, who had served in a transport company responsible for the transport of fuel and food to the front line. He even knew that when the *Wehrmacht* invaded Russia in 1941 with more than three million troops, there were 750.000 draught and riding horses in the three army groups.

I went to bed and couldn't sleep for quite a while what with all the new impressions of the day.

The other two members of our *Festigungsbrigade,* Dagmar and Wilfried, told me later that their *Neubauern* were resettlers as they were called in East Germany, in order to avoid the term "homeland expellees" for the 12 million Germans who had during and shortly after the war been expelled from various Eastern countries or what were formerly parts of Germany.

Of course, when I spent my week at Albin's, I was hardly aware of all the following details.

About 4 million of the 12 million evacuees settled in East Germany, making up about 24 percent of the population. The largest portion went to West Germany, where they formed about 15 percent of the inhabitants. To get an idea of the magnitude of this migration and resettlement after the war, it should be remembered that East Germany was about the size of Virginia and had a population of 18 million, about 3 million more than the Carolinas.

Today Germany is quite a bit smaller than California (357,000 km² as compared to 424,000 km²) but has 82 million residents as compared to California's 37 million.

This is to say that the task of integrating 12 million refugees into a Germany that had lost 25 percent of its territory was huge but, after the initial enmity from the old populace, which feared for their rights and property, in the end was managed quite well in both parts of Germany. Needless to say, all the newcomers from the East pretended to have been ardent antifascists.

Since the big cities were largely destroyed by bombs, it seemed a matter of course that as many as possible were settled in the rural areas, in East Germany alone about 210,000 receiving farm land.

It was still dark when we had breakfast the next morning with Ingrid having prepared it, and a light early morning mist lay over the farmyard and the adjoining fields. Albin, after having fed and watered the horses, harnessed them to the potato digger and out we went, the sun just visible above the horizon. He sat on the iron saddle of the digger while I went behind, picking up the potatoes and throwing them in piles, which we would later haul from the field to the barn. Every half hour we took turns and Albin collected the potatoes while

I proudly sat on the digger and after some initial clumsiness did quite well, at least Albin told me so. He said not to work too hard with the picking, as later in the day some women from the village, being remunerated in kind with potatoes, along with his wife Ingrid and even Kilian would do most of this work, which, Albin said, was not meant to be done by men.

So the week went by, and in the breaks and evenings I learned piecemeal of Albin's experiences, opinions and expectations. His sorrows and complaints were as follows.

In 1957, Nikita Khrushchev visited the German Democratic Republic. This Soviet half-literate statesman, who in the United Nations General Assembly on October 12, 1960 took one of his shoes off and in protest hammered with it on the table didn't hammer when visiting East Germany but said a few ludicrous words concerning the cultivation of corn while visiting a collective. Walking through corn fields with his East German comrades-in-arms he said, holding a particularly large corn cob in his hand: "This is the wurst on the stem," of course in his Ukrainian-colored Russian. Now one must know that every fart let loose in the Soviet Union was in the German Democratic Republic taken as God's word. So, God having departed, the Party at once began a campaign for the quick extension of corn cultivation, notwithstanding soil properties, microclimate, digestibility of silage corn for pigs, availability of silos, and experiences of the farmers. Those who raised concerns were decried, as an article Albin gave me from the *Leipziger Volkszeitung* illustrates:

"Corn cultivation has become a political question of great significance, which must be discussed with the utmost sharpness. We hereby ask chief agronomist Ehrenburg of the Machine-and-Tractor-Station Dölzig why he is against it and recommends slowing down on corn growing. Nobody must be spared; everybody must take a clear position ... This also refers to comrade Löffelbein, member of the committee of experts with the Council of the District of Leipzig and research assistant at the Agricultural Research Farm Oberholz, who wrongly contends that corn silage is unsuitable for feeding pigs and will lead to digestive disorders.

The members of the District *(Bezirk)* Parliament also may no longer be silent about this important question. We are certain that in their next session they will find out why their decisions have not been put into practice. Those who are guilty have questions to answer. If Comrade Khrushchev during his visit said that here grows the wurst on the stem, it means this is not only a technical, but in the first place a political issue which must be dealt with accordingly ...

And it must never be forgotten that the enforcement of corn cultivation reflects the class struggle between the old capitalist and the new socialist order ... There are still many political doubts, but they will be overcome. But we must not forget that our adversaries have their fingers in the pie and want to prevent an increase in corn production. Therefore, any further discussions of corn cultivation should begin with the sentence: Tell me what your attitude is toward corn cultivation and I can tell you who you are."

After I had read the article Albin had given me, he looked at me sadly and said: "You can now see my problem. The *LPG* chairman, who is an old friend of my family, told me the other day how the county is pestering him about the increase of corn production, though he had repeatedly tried to explain to them that our soil and climate will never yield the expected corn crop, and it is a waste of time, labor and resources to insist on extending corn growing. If I were a full member of the *LPG,* I would have no say in which crop to cultivate on my fields and would have to comply with any nonsense the Party comes up with."

I was silent. What can one say considering such idiocy? But worse was to come, when Albin began to talk about the Open Cowshed Policy, which stipulated that livestock should be kept in open stalls all year round, the introduction of which had been demanded by the 33rd plenary session of the Central Committee of the Socialist Unity Party in 1957. In his main speech the then Secretary-General of the Party, Walter Ulbricht, who had learned the trade of a joiner before becoming a full-time communist functionary, never having had anything to do with agriculture, styled this form of cattle husbandry as a socialist achievement of the highest order and an indispensable requirement for "further improving the living standard of the people" (in fact for overcoming serious food supply problems East Germany faced in the late fifties due to the socialist transformation of agriculture).

Now principally, Albin said, in the summer cows and other cattle can and even should be kept in open stables or sheds, where they can seek shelter against rain, storm and sun. It only so happened that the comrades from the Secretary-General downward to the County Party organization seemed to have forgotten that in the *Vogtland* region and elsewhere in East Germany there are quite harsh winters with temperature of minus 15 to 20 °C (5 to minus 4 °F). The county vet had informed him that the udders of many cows had frozen to the dung they were standing in and the cows had then to be emergency slaughtered.

With a bitter laugh Albin showed me another cutting with the beautiful and enticing slogan:

Steht die Kuh im Offenstall,
wird das Euter dick und prall.

A cow that stands in open stall
Has udder full with milk for all.

I later learned that it took state and Party about two years to remedy the situation and add walls to the open stables and make them winterproof, not before 720 cows had died daily until 1959/60. In the meantime hundreds of farmers had fled to West Germany via the still open frontier with West Berlin or the loosely guarded "green border", often slaughtering their farm animals before and taking with them the century-old expertise of their forefathers, the knowledge of the locality and the intimate connection between the farmer and his land and livestock, thereby increasing the shortage of farm labor.

Of course, the keeping of cows in open stables had likewise been declared a political question by the Party and any who dared voice concerns were threatened.

Albin pointed out that had he been a full member of the Waldhausen collective at the time of the open cowshed frenzy his eight cows, all of whom he called by name, would probably have frozen to death or been prematurely slaughtered.

His third main reason for wanting to remain a private farmer had to do with the raising of pigs. He showed me his ten pigs in their sty and the flap door, which allowed them to roam outside in a fenced kind of mud yard. And then he told me of the plan the government had for the mass rearing of pigs. 100,000 pigs were to be reared near Waldhausen in an area which bordered a nature preserve with fish ponds, game preserves and hiking paths. The idea was of course to produce on an industrial scale as much pork for export to West Germany as possible without regard to animal welfare, nature protection, air and water pollution and so on. Pig or rather pork as an export article had a great advantage in that it was paid for immediately by the buyer, so that the GDR could get the urgently needed hard currency quickly if necessary, which was often the case. Do you know, Albin asked me, what amount of feed 100,000 pigs need daily? 300 tons. Do you know how much manure they produce daily? 3000 cubic meters or 3 million liters. This is more than the 500,000 residents of Leipzig generate in a day. And can you imagine what the managers do with the manure they can't process in the planned sewage plants? Of course, discharge it into the rivers or spread it on the fields in a much too high amount to be tolerable for the ground water. No, my student friend, Albin said, I want no part of all that. Either they leave me alone or I know what to do. He didn't explain that but I guessed what he meant and felt deeply sorry for him. During my short stay with him I had seen how much he identified himself with the land and the livestock and how much his heart hung on everything connected with it. One of his fellow farmers, who was not a New Farmer but whose family had been in possession of their land for generations, had been more pragmatic and had said to him: There was once the Kaiser's empire, there was once Hitler's empire and yet everything changed again. We just want to hold on and wait for what's going to come next year.

One time in our talks we had a good laugh when Albin told me how he had silenced a functionary from the *LPG* by demanding the immediate implementation of communism rather than just socialism—claiming that just as the workers were given complete factories (accordingly called People's Own Factory) so would he enter the *LPG* once the state had constructed the new livestock sheds (which he was sure they hadn't the capability of doing for years to come). Then we got serious again when Albin told me of a friend in Thuringia who due to the constant "persuasion" by the police, Stasi and brigades of agitation had committed suicide, leaving a note that he could no longer withstand the pressure.

The week had passed more quickly than I would have liked, and on the last day, a Saturday, we said good-bye not before promising that we would stay in touch, which didn't somehow work out. A car from the county came with Wilfried and Dagmar already in it and picked me up.

All the students of the *Festigungsbrigaden,* about 50, were gathered together in the *Kulturhaus* Karl-Marx-Stadt for a final evaluation of the heroic undertaking in favor of socialist agriculture. Before we went in, I talked to Elisabeth and Heike, two fellow students of mine, who looked rather subdued. Asked what was wrong they told me about their week as *Festigungsbrigade.* When they had arrived at their village and gone into the mayor's office to find out where to go, the mayor, a good-natured man, had said: Girls, I can't send you to the farmers. When word got around that you would come and would campaign for the *LPG,* some farmers threatened they would set their dogs on you, and others said they would chase you away with pitchforks. Therefore, you will stay here and help me with my overwhelming paperwork. And this was what they did. And now they were afraid of what was ahead of them for not having met the Party's expectations.

Then the assembly started.

Functionaries from Halle University and from the Karl-Marx-Stadt District Party Office sat at a long table on a kind of elevated platform while we students sat in the auditorium. The agricultural secretary of the Party gave a longish speech, principally praising our commitment, which, he said, could of course not be measured in numbers, but would certainly have a long-term effect. At the end he regretted to say that some of us had not fulfilled the Party's expectations. He looked at a paper in front of him and called out a name, my name. This student, he said, instead of conducting political talks with his farmer, had worked with him and thus helped him to stay outside the cooperative. I gathered all my courage, stood up and said that I couldn't possibly convince my farmer without sharing some of his work. And now a small miracle set in: One of the comrades on the platform, obviously having higher authority than the agricultural secretary, announced that Comrade Werner, me, (I wasn't even a member of the Party, a "comrade"), was quite right. How can you talk to a farmer and not know anything about his work?

The agricultural secretary was silenced, for the moment, but then took his revenge. He called out the names of Elisabeth and Heike, certain that the poor girls were too shy to answer him in public, and said that they had worked in the mayor's office and not talked to the farmers. Was this not, he barked, a sure sign of ideological watering down of the Party's efforts? Did this not open the door to the class enemy to get in and prevent collectivization, a process to which the Party had dedicated all its efforts? Should one not ask if those two girls were still worthy of studying at a socialist university? Dead silence everywhere. Of course, Elisabeth and Heike were too frightened to justify themselves and to tell how it came about that they had stayed in the mayor's office. Fortunately, nothing detrimental happened to them afterwards, though the rest of us had to live with the uneasy knowledge that we had remained silent, having failed to speak up. And it was not to be the last time either.

We went home to resume our studies and followed the consolidation of the collectives in the newspapers, knowing it had not been affected by us but through the State's coercion.

Decades later, after the fall of the Wall in 1989, I got a letter from Kilian Schröter. Soon after everybody in the village had joined the cooperative, his father had relented too and had even gotten to a leading post in the *LPG*'s cattle breeding section. He lived to see the end of the GDR and got his farm back. He and other farmers of the village subsequently formed a large cooperative, now under capitalist conditions, and were doing quite well. He, Kilian himself, had studied agriculture at—yes, at Halle university, my old *alma mater*, and was now working in his father's cooperative. The industrial pig farm with a hundred thousand pigs had indeed been built with all the dire consequences for the animals, the environment and the farm laborers Albin had predicted, but was immediately dismantled after the end of the communist regime.

In a footnote Kilian had added that after some years in the *LPG* his parents were quite content. They enjoyed something like an eight-hour-day, unthinkable as private farmers, could cultivate a patch of field near their house and also keep poultry and two pigs for their own purposes in addition to the fixed wages they got from the cooperative. Life was easier and their material living standard was higher, which they regarded as an acceptable compensation for the loss of their status as private farmers. They particularly profited from the system of "free peaks", that is excess production beyond the state quota for which the state was willing to pay a higher price.

I am still asking myself today how big my impact as a member of a *Festigungsbrigade* was on the collectivization of farming or agriculture as a whole in the German Democratic Republic or even in the socialist world system. Did I even prolong its existence, God forbid, by a nanosecond?

3 GOD BE WITH YOU

For what happened in the year of the Lord 1978 I must blame myself, well, at least partly. I was between wives, sort of, as I was still living with my first wife, but casting my eyes about for a new and hopefully happier partnership.

The situation in the German Democratic Republic had gradually gotten worse regarding the freedom of expression, the dissemination of information, and the ability to travel to name just the three that were most important to me. My job as a lecturer of English at a Technical University was moving into the sphere of the ridiculous since I had never been allowed to visit an English-speaking country, nor could I hope to ever get to one. To be fair: we had a kind of on the job training in the form of summer courses with native speakers from England, most of them well-meaning leftists half blind to the socialist reality in the GDR, who did what they could to make dents into our stilted, academic, puristic and grammar-oriented approach to the English language.

In my teaching job at the college, which included crash courses for engineers, scientists, managers and others from industrial enterprises and academic institutions, it occurred more often than I liked that some of the people I was teaching had actually been to England or the USA on business trips. And they brought with them words, phrases, idioms, dialects, technical words and so on which were new to me. I remember that one of them told the group about his trip to New York, where he had had the chance to take a boat ride in New York

Harbor. A boat ride, for heaven's sake. How can you ride a boat? I queried. In my obviously outdated understanding you rode horses, or maybe bicycles, even hobby horses, but not a boat. What you did were take boat trips. But the man, a *Reisekader*, as people were called who were allowed to go on official trips to capitalist countries, insisted that he had taken part in a boat ride, and even paid for it in dollars. He shouldn't have mentioned the payment, as he had spent precious hard currency (which had been given him by his generous host, an energy company in New Jersey for a paper he had read there) for his personal pleasure instead of saving the money and handing it in to the government after his return, as was the strict order in the GDR.

This sin against the holy spirit of socialism had been duly noted by a Stasi informant in the class. Consequently, he was, he told me later when I met him by chance, reprimanded by his director and the party secretary and lost his *Reisekader* status. That's what happens! To my shame I felt a tiny bit of schadenfreude. This same man had also told the group of new developments in American orthography, of which I had never heard. He had seen billboards and advertisements with the spelling of lite and nite instead of light and night. God help us, I thought, what is my beloved English degenerating to? The language of Shakespeare, Dickens, Galsworthy, Greene, Hemingway, Dreiser, Sinclair and a few others on which we had been fed as students? And even worse, he asked me what kind of English was I teaching since he, wanting to buy a hot dog in the street, could only make himself understood by pointing his finger at the desired product. The vendor had finally told him that he was selling something that he called hoddog, pronounced almost like huddog. And what about the phrase I had taught them about being offered a bag by the clerk at check-out? "Would you like to have a bag?" What the clerks said was something like "Wanna bag?" And not just once had he heard that, but most of the time. No mention of the word "do" in the question. Hardly ever had he (and other *Reisekaders*) heard something like "Where do you come from?" How much time have we wasted on the grammatically correct form of English questions? Instead they were confronted with the alien form "Where you from?" How can they go on trusting my English, he implied?

It is understandable that under these circumstances I tried to find consolation other than in my job. Such a consolation offered itself in the form of a pretty course member, female, who was not unappreciative of my friendly words when we had a beer in the canteen celebrating our mid-course event. We ended up in her room in the student dormitory, where the course members had been given accommodation. As I am, even by my enemies, regarded as tactful and discreet, I cannot say here how I enjoyed the night. This enjoyment went on for the rest of the course (which was a three-week undertaking), though ended in a great shock for me. On the last day, after handing out the certificates of attendance including some kind of assessment (needless to say that the pretty woman had passed as one of the best), we wanted to say good-bye and find some way of further communicating with each other, on the sly, of course, when suddenly her husband appeared to pick her up and take her home. He was a really huge guy, and, as I was told by other participants, heavy weight boxing champion of the district or county of Magdeburg. Of this decisive fact the pretty woman had kept me unaware. I of course abandoned all thoughts of further communication with her. But obviously that did not teach me enough. In another course, a year later, my political frustration still going strong, another husband turned out to be a lieutenant of the Ministry for State Security, the *Stasi*. Now here I experienced what can be called a close shave.

He must have divined that something was wrong with his wife, maybe she was a bit short with him on the telephone, or she did not say often enough that she loved him. Or talked too well about her charming English instructor. Anyway, in the end, when he came to take her home, he said he wanted to have a word with me. Now in this case it wasn't his size, which was roughly the same as mine, but his job that sort of took me aback. He did not hesitate to disclose it to me.

At that time the German Democratic Republic, East Germany, had a population of roughly 17 million (which is less than e. g. half the 37 million Californians). It used to be more than 19 million in 1946, but more than two million had preferred to leave the promised socialist land for the rough winds of the capitalist West, since 1949 known as the Federal Republic of Germany, for short, West Germany.

The Ministry for State Security (also State Security Service), which was formed after the Soviet example of the "Cheka" (The All-Russian Emergency Commission for Combating Counter-Revolution and Sabotage) up to its very end harbored Stalinist ideas about what the practice of socialism/communism should be like. It employed about 91,000 people full-time, including 2,000 fully employed unofficial collaborators, 13,073 soldiers and 2,232 officers of the GDR army along with 173,000 unofficial informants inside the country and 1,550 informants in West Germany. If you break this down to how many people observed, told upon, investigated, destroyed, blackmailed, threatened, opened letters, tapped telephone conversations and tried to keep in constant fear the 17 million GDR citizens, you arrive at the astonishing number of one *Stasi* person per 64 GDR residents. Now compare this to the 36,000 full-time employees the FBI is said to have to watch over 323 million Americans, 1 FBI person per 9,000 people. The number of spies or informants in FBI pay seems to be a closely guarded secret, some sources say it is 15,000 plus another 45,000 not officially listed.

The Stasi also had at its disposal the Felix Dzerzhinsky Guards Regiment; the armed force named after the founder of the Cheka. They were responsible for protecting government and party buildings and personnel. The regiment, with nearly 11,000 soldiers virtually a division, was composed of six motorized rifle battalions, one artillery battalion, and one training battalion. Its equipment included armored personnel carriers, 120 mm mortars, 85 mm and 100 mm antitank guns, anti-aircraft guns, helicopters and armored cars for riot control.

The *Stasi* was not just a secret service, but also an official investigative authority for political and related crimes with its own prisons, academies and a foreign intelligence department.

We were of course not aware of the exact size of this formidable force, which was just as well, because our ignorance prevented us from living in the constant fear which the *Stasi* tried to create.

Now about the *Stasi* husband-lieutenant. He looked me hard in the eye and told me what he would and could do to me if I ever came near his wife again. The GDR was at that time in a period of detente with West Germany, which the husband did not seem to realize. Though some things were getting worse, others were not. Party and state leader Erich Honecker had for quite a time been doing everything in his power to get himself an invitation by the West German chancellor Helmut Kohl to visit West Germany, thus hoping to get more of a recognition for East Germany in the Western World. Kohl of course set certain conditions, like for example easing up on political repression in the GDR. So looking back at the enraged husband—his wife standing nearby looking shy and afraid, which increased her prettiness—I said that he should not get paranoid, and as he could see from his wife's course assessment, she had had no time for any escapades and anyway was a much too loyal a partner to cheat on him. And by God, Mielke's (the *Stasi* minister's) faithful soldier believed me, or rather wanted to believe me in order to protect his *Stasi* manhood and even said good-bye in English, not knowing of course that this expression derives from the old phrase "God be with you".

The *Stasi* saw itself as, and really was, an absolutely loyal servant of the Communist Party. This went so far that its agents abroad, who were often secretly members of the Party, had to pay their monthly membership fees. As proof of that their controllers or case officers in East Berlin stuck the verifying stamps into their membership booklets and noted it on special lists, which contained the agents' code names, transaction numbers and sums of money (the amount of which depending on their West German, that is capitalist, salaries). When Werner Stiller, a *Stasi* first lieutenant, defected to the West in 1979 bringing with him a trove of material from the *Stasi* headquarters including some of these lists (recounted in his book *Der Agent*), West German counter-intelligence, with the help of code names and transaction numbers, was able to identify and bring to trial East German agents who had long been active in the West.

Incidentally, Stiller's girl-friend, who had helped him escape, was on the point of being arrested in the Thuringian city of Oberhof, where she was working as a waitress, when the hard winter of 1979 with much snow and ice covering roads prevented the *Stasi* from getting to Oberhof from Berlin headquarters in time because they had no winter tires, which were, as many things in the country, in short supply. Their helicopter was not operational, either. So she escaped to Warsaw, got into the West German embassy and was flown out to West Germany. God and the socialist economy had helped her.

4 Blessings of a Planned Economy

Growing up, I had a lot of uncles, my mother and father each having had three brothers. One of them, my father's brother, a surgeon major, went missing before Moscow in the Second World War, another had lost his right leg in Russia, which fascinated us children because we were allowed to knock on his wooden prothesis, to which he usually answered "ouch". Even more fascinating was the pain he was still feeling in his foot that lay somewhere on the banks of the Dnieper on the steppes of the Ukraine. So we wondered if this foot was perhaps still alive and walking around. I even dreamed once that it had entered my room at night and demanded to be reconnected to its leg.

Another uncle was said to have served in the *Feld-gendarmerie*, the dreaded military police of the *Wehrmacht,* which had committed atrocities in Russia and other occupied countries. But this was only whispered in the family, and when I asked his widow after his death about his activity in the army, she said he had just been a member of the NSKK, the National Socialist Motor Corps, which was a training organization of the Nazi Party. With the outbreak of World War II NSKK ranks were recruited to serve in the transport corps of various German military branches. So it may well be that this uncle had been to Russia, too. What he had done there he took with him to his grave.

With one of my uncles I had a special relationship. Before and during the war he had served in the merchant navy. His ship was bombed or hit a mine in the Baltic and sunk. With the help of a wooden plank he kept himself above the water for a few hours until he was rescued by another ship. Since the water was so cold, his testicles virtually disappeared into his body, but, as he slyly told me, came down after he got warm again and served him well in his later life. He had three children, my cousins. This uncle was born in 1922 and thus belonged to the Stalingrad generation, which like no other vintage was decimated in the Second World War. Luckily as a merchant sailor he was not recruited into the army. Maybe this kind of luck was one of the reasons for his extreme sense of humor, which did not leave him even when he was dying in 2009, at the age of 87.

On his deathbed he asked his daughters for a telephone and rang his sister, my mother, then 96 years old, and told her that he was dying and please not to come visiting in order not to increase the turmoil around his bed. My mother, incidentally, had a similar kind of stoicism. When she was dying with three of her children around her bed, my grandson, her great grandson, 4 years old, asked in the stillness of the room: "Great Granny, are you now dying?". My mother looked at him with her half sightless eyes and said: "Yes, my dear, now I am dying."

After the war my uncle returned to his birthplace Aschersleben at the foot of the Harz mountains and, still being young, had the pleasure to outlive the Soviet Occupation Zone, the German Democratic Republic and finally to end up in reunified Germany. Here he enjoyed for almost another 20 years the generous pension that the West

German chancellor Helmut Kohl included in the German Reunification Treaty of 1990 for all GDR old-age pensioners (who had not been able to contribute to the statutory West German pension scheme but now benefited from it).

I liked him a lot and often asked him to tell me about his experiences as a metal worker, an engineer and finally the head of the investment department of the *WEMA*, the *Werkzeugmaschinenfabrik* (machine-tool factory) Aschersleben.

First of all, he gave me to understand the intricacies of the socialist economy, which were of course different from the ones I experienced in the educational system. For everything in the centrally planned economy, also called command economy by mean-spirited critics, be it produced or consumed, there were fixed amounts. Resources were allocated, which is understandable, but also consumption figures were planned and fixed in the five-year plans long before the population started to consume the specific product, and woe to those who wanted to consume, buy or otherwise get hold of things that were not planned. The planning was done in the State Planning Commission, which had its branches in the districts (lands), counties and towns. Shirts or bras and knickers could only be produced as predetermined in Berlin or the regional or local planning commissions, houses be built likewise and so on.

It is not for fun that I am mentioning bras and knickers. My uncle told me that for some unknown reason in the city of Jena bras were in short supply. Maybe too many husbands in their lust had torn them off their wives unplanned and tried to get too hastily into their knickers. Anyway, in the eighties of the last century female workers of the big *VEB Carl Zeiss Jena* factory complained to the director-general that they could not get hold of decent underwear, or if such were to be had, the workers usually arrived too late at the shops after work, when the underwear was sold out. So, the director-general, a member of the influential Central Committee of the Socialist Unity Party *SED*, the Communist Party, and the virtual ruler of the city of Jena, spent some of the precious hard currency of his optical works to import female underwear from West Germany. Thus it happened that good-humored women in the streets of Jena asked each other what they were wearing under their pullovers. Not a capitalist bra, I trust? Of course, the import did not last long and they had to return to a more practical and at the same time very durable fashion again. The said director-general was much applauded for his heroic deed.

When my uncle told me this, I could add something from my own life in the city of Halle. One day my tooth-brush broke and I ran to the drug-store to buy a new one. Out of stock, they told me. I ran to a pharmacist, out of stock, he said. I ran to the next supermarket, same answer. I went to work feeling very uncomfortable with my uncleaned teeth. There I learned from a usually well-informed Party member that a batch of plastic had been ruined in the chemical factory of Leuna, which was the raw material for tooth-brushes. In the whole district of Halle, you could not buy any tooth-brushes. As a consequence, a number of people went on sick leave claiming they could not go to work with uncleaned teeth.

Now the government or rather Party in Berlin, learning of the shame, frantically imported, unscheduled in the national economic plan, tooth-brushes. For this they had to export a bigger amount of pork, which again caused, though only temporarily, a shortage of pork. The tooth-brush calamity only lasted for a few days, and I could take pride in the fact that for a time I scrubbed my communist teeth with a capitalist tooth-brush, though I did not feel any difference.

Here my uncle reminded me of the shortage of toilet paper that occurred sometime in the seventies. Nobody knew the reasons for this, could it have been an unplanned outbreak of diarrhoea, commonly known as the runs, more graphically called *Dünnschiss* in German? I remembered that we rushed to the supermarkets and apothecaries to buy tissue, which was only on sale in big packets, consisting of unwieldy lengths. So, at home you had to cut the lengths to manageable pieces. At least people did not have to resort to newspapers, cut to rectangular bits as we did shortly after the war.

I recently read that if the East German government had listened to the then Polish government spokesman Jerzy Urban's somewhat cynical idea, they would not have arrived at the described calamity. Jerzy Urban had calculated that there was usually only a 10% shortage of toilet paper. But these few percentages led the people to hoarding or panic buying of this if not precious then indispensable commodity. The same happened, by the way, to car spare parts in East Germany. I, for one used to have at least the following spare parts for my Trabant car in the garage: a rear-view mirror, a complete exhaust system, a fan belt, several spark plugs, two spare tires, two sets of lamps for head- and tail-lights and two windscreen wipers. No wonder these parts were not on sale in the shops, if most people stored them in their garages. Back to the Polish proposal. If, Urban suggested, the width of the toilet paper roll was reduced by 10%, hardly noticeable in daily usage, one could put the people at rest, avoid hoarding and increase the popularity of Party and government. Perhaps Urban's idea was not cynical at all?

But my uncle topped all that by remembering what came to be known as the coffee crisis in 1977. To understand its impact, one must know that you could do a lot to folks in socialist Germany without them seriously revolting. You could anger them with the monotonous censured newspapers, let them wait for 10 to 15 years for a car, refuse them visits to western countries (as long as they could go to sunny Bulgaria or to Hungary, called the happiest barrack in the socialist camp), even have them listen to the boring speeches of members of the Politburo or have them coping for a few days without toilet paper, but taking away their coffee break at work or their afternoon coffee over weekends at home was an unforgivable sin, which could lead to serious political upheavals.

The coffee crisis actually began in 1976. The price of coffee rose dramatically after a failed harvest in Brazil, forcing the government to spend approximately 700 million West German Deutschmarks on coffee per year (approximately 300 million US dollars, equivalent to $1.19 billion today), nearly five times the planned 150 million West German Deutschmarks. Now the Party leadership desperately tried to make up for this by having their coffee specialists create a new brand called *Kaffee-Mix*, a mixture of 50% genuine coffee and 50% ersatz coffee. This *Kaffee-Mix* soon came to be called *Erichs Krönung* (Erich's Crowning), a reference to Erich Honecker, the party and state leader, and the West German *Jacobs Krönung* coffee brand. This very quickly alerted the *Stasi* secret service and political police, who did not fail to report it to Berlin. There they did not react immediately, hoping that the population would acquire their coffee from West German relatives. This increased the demand for the typical return gift, *Dresdener Stollen*, a very popular sweet cake in Germany formed like a loaf of bread, eaten before, at and after Christmas. Since there are indispensable ingredients in the Stollen such as almonds, raisins and saccade without which no decent German housewife would bake a *Stollen*, and which also needed to be bought abroad for hard currency, the snake bit its own tail. The *Kaffee-Mix* damaged the coffee machines at factory canteens as it contained substitute ingredients such as pea flour, which has proteins that swell under heat and pressure thus clogging the filters, which again had to be produced unplanned.

Though the West German relatives did what they could for their relations in the East, and it was estimated that 20 to 25% of the entire coffee drank in East Germany came from the West through private channels, it was not enough. The government had to back-paddle and return to the import of palatable coffee, which in the end hastened the decline of the East German economy. One good thing arose from the coffee crisis, albeit not for the East Germans, but for the befriended Republic of Vietnam. Trying to avoid coffee crises in the future, the East German government signed treaties with Vietnam stipulating that East Germany provide the necessary equipment and machinery for coffee production and Vietnam increase the area for coffee plantations and provide the necessary workforce, for which East Germany was to build houses, hospitals and shops. Against these investments, which included a hydropower plant, East Germany was to receive half of the coffee harvest for the next 20 years. As it happened, when the coffee plants, taking 8 years until the first usable harvest, yielded the first coffee beans in 1990, the German Democratic Republic was disappearing. But Vietnam was able to establish itself as the second-largest coffee producer in the world after Brazil. In particular this helped the improvement of trade relations between the U.S. and Vietnam. So, Americans, when you drink your admittedly weak coffee, don't forget whom you have, at least partly, to thank but please without unnecessary coyness.

My uncle told me about his work as head of the investment department of the machine-tool factory. Since the key figures of the Planning Commission with regard to resources and requirements hardly ever were realistic but mostly wishful thinking, my uncle's only way—a tightrope walk between success and punishment—to allegedly have fulfilled the investment plan was to distort the figures, disguise the real situation, report wrong delivery times, lie to the authorities and so on. But somehow, since he went unpunished, he seems to have succeeded. Not everybody had so much luck, or cleverness. It was told on the grapevine, maybe as a warning, that the chairman of a county in the district of Potsdam, disregarding the central plan that had budgeted the allocation of resources for a different project, in this case a building for the County Party Organization, had used it to build an indoor swimming pool for the population. The work was not yet finished when he was arrested, brought to trial and sentenced to some years in prison, the accusation being "offences against the socialist economy". The swimming pool was finished sometime later, much praised by the people and the schools, which could now give their pupils swimming instruction the year round. This did not really help the imprisoned chairman, though it might have consoled him a bit.

An interesting example of economic creativity was the children's holiday camp, which every *Volkseigener Betrieb, VEB*, (publicly owned company) was obliged to build and organize. But such camps were hardly ever included in the state plans. This meant that all building materials, ground, labor force etc. had to be provided outside the economic plan, this sacred cow. Thus, my uncle and his men had to work so to say outside or against the law that the plan constituted. They found a suitable location near Lake Müritz in the north-east of the country. First my uncle armed himself with a case of large bottles of *Nordhäuser Korn*, which is a colorless distilled beverage produced from fermented cereal grain seed, rye or wheat. *Korn* differs from vodka in that it is distilled to lower alcoholic proof and less rigorously filtered, which leaves more of the cereal grain flavor in the finished spirit.

Above 37.5% ABV (75 proof) it may be named *Kornbrand*, and the name *Doppelkorn*, with 38% ABV (76 proof), has been used in the market. The latter is to be recommended to all who love a good spirit and also love to be in good spirits. My uncle also took along several cartons of high-quality cigarettes and a deer, shot in the Harz mountains and illegally obtained by him. Thus equipped he drove to a timber company near the camp location and exchanged his loot for prefabricated bungalow parts and the promise that children of this company could also attend the holiday camp. By similar semi-criminal acts, he and his team from the investment department in Aschersleben were able to get hold of the required backhoe, transformer station, concrete, installations for the showers, the kitchen and everything else needed for a camp.

The workers came from the factory in Aschersleben and took turns every two weeks. Those remaining at home did their work for them. Of course, in the camp they worked more hours than was legally allowed, but the trade union officials looked away or worked with them, because it was always a nice outing, away from the wives despite the hard labor they had to do. They finished their work in time for the children to enjoy their holidays there, but my uncle had made one mistake. They had built a jetty on the nearby bank of Lake Müritz for the four row boats that he had managed to procure from a Berlin boatyard. He had not made an application for the jetty at the waterways authority and thus was not entitled to build the jetty. He had to pay a fine of 300 GDR marks, which was relatively mild. Of course, the money for the

Nordhäuser Korn, the fine, the cigarettes he took out of his own pocket. The deer he got in exchange for smoked eel that he had gotten from an acquaintance near Rostock on the Baltic, who needed fittings for his bathroom, which my uncle had been able to channel off from the fittings for the holiday camp.

I think the reader can now better understand how the East Germany economy could function in spite of its inherent shortcomings: through the initiative and energy of people like my uncle, of whose kind there were many in the country always working on a tight rope from which they could easily fall.

But it was not only vile material goods that were exchanged on the grey market. I had a friend who was a lecturer of Russian at a nearby university. He wanted gas heating in his flat because he would no longer carry lignite up three flights of stairs for his heating. He contacted a plumber, a tradesman always much in demand and difficult to get hold of, who needed a Russian language certificate in order to take part in a training scheme in the Soviet Union, for which this language certificate was required. My friend wrote the necessary Russian essay for him and, with the help of a colleague, who signed the essay and the mock minutes of the oral examination as a second examiner, created credible exam documentation, which his gullible head of department signed, knowing him as an honest soul. The second examiner did my friend this favor without a material reward, just for the sake of her very intimate friendship with him. When my friend wanted to pay the plumber for his work, this equally honest man only wanted to be paid for his work hours, because, as he said, he had brought all the pipes, gadgets, valves and so on "free" as he said, from his place of work.

Another example of the relationship economy was connected with my broken Trabant windshield. I went to the publicly-owned repair shop, only to be told that they had no windshields. Luckily, I had a brother-in-law who was a trombonist and a double bass player at the Halle municipal theater's Handel orchestra (Halle on the Saale river is the birthplace of the famous composer). Beside his work at the theater he had time to manage a group of theater musicians who made popular music for events outside the theater. When the manager of this car repair shop celebrated his 50th birthday, they engaged my brother-in-law's group for the music. The manager thanked the group profusely and somewhat carelessly, saying to my brother-in-law that whenever he needed something, he could always come to him for help. So my brother-in-law rang him and told him that he now had the chance of fulfilling his promise. This the manager did, found a windshield (which, as he had first told me they did not have), installed it and said good-bye to me with a sweet-sour smile because he had been under the impression that his promise was to my brother-in-law, not for his relatives.

The translation of words which designate a phenomenon unique to one culture into another language is at best a difficult business and in many cases nearly impossible. The easiest way is to use the word in its original form, as is the case with German words like *angst* and *schadenfreude* in

English. Now these words and the phenomena described by them are very common, which is not the case with the word *Bückware*. It is a kind of satirical expression for goods (*Ware*) for which one has to stoop down (*sich bücken*) to obtain them. In most cases, however, it was the shop assistant who stooped down behind their counter to get hold of an article they had wisely hidden because it was in short supply. And the assistant had saved it for acquaintances, friends or people from whom they could expect another rare article in return.

To be historically correct, *Bückware* originates from Nazi times and is said to have come into use at the beginning of the Second World War, when things started to become scarce. Later in West Germany it was used, rarely, for things you wanted to buy unnoticed, like pornographic journals. But in East Germany its usage was revived and used for all things difficult to buy, and there were many, among them bananas, spare parts for cars, electrical hand drills, certain books, linen, certain beer brands like *Radeberger Pils,* calf's liver, oranges, woodchip wallpaper, jeans, etc.

Some of the articles mentioned lost their status of *Bückware* from time to time when the government decided to produce a sufficient quantity or increase the import, e. g. of oranges. State and Party leader Erich Honecker had a few million Westmarks at his personal disposal and could play Father Christmas in December and buy products in West Germany like oranges and sometimes even bananas. But Christmas being over, particularly bananas returned to their original status of *Bückware*. Smoked eel that I mentioned above was not *Bückware,* because the shop assistant could stoop behind their counter as often as they wished but could not produce it. It simply was not on the market, because it was exported for hard currency. The only way it could be obtained was if you were lucky enough to have a friend who operated a smoke-house behind his house where he smoked eels for himself and maybe close friends, though he was not allowed to sell them legally. Everybody knew that you could not buy smoked eel, so the joke went: A customer enters a fish shop and asks for smoked eel. Out of stock, he is told. He complains how can that be. The assistant asks him to wait a bit and serves numerous other customers. The shop being empty again, he turns to the eel lover and asks: Have you seen anybody asking for smoked eel? No. So why should we stock it?

Bizarre things happened in the planned economy. For example, bed linen was hardly ever on display in the shops. But the people's linen cupboards were full, and freshly married couples got a rich dowry in the form of bedclothes. But since the rumor went around that bed linen was scarce, people bought it ahead and so caused shortage. Same with other products. Or let's say a family in a small town prepared a big family get-together and bought a larger quantity of beverages, normally in stock. Other customers accidentally observing the purchase assumed there was a shortage ahead and consequently also bought the beverage to stock it at home. A chain reaction started that then led to a real shortage on the market. And the clumsy economic planning was hardly ever able to react quickly enough, e. g. by diverting things from other places to the needy one.

Without doubt in the course of its limited life from 1949 to 1989 the German Democratic Republic became a country of tinkerers and inventors, not because of a special German inventiveness (which cannot entirely be denied as the history of technology and natural sciences shows), but because the socialist economy of scarcity demanded permanent contemplation about how one could best muddle through in the face of the shortage of so many goods. When the fan belt of my Trabant car broke during a trip to the Baltic, I remembered the advice of a friend and asked my wife to remove her tights, which I then knotted around the V-belt pulleys and so was able to continue our trip to the next repair shop. Needless to say, the shop could not help me with the belt. Out of stock. But my wife had a sufficient number of tights in her luggage, which saw us to the Baltic and back home, where I had, see above, a spare belt in my garage. I have to admit that I felt a certain kick driving a car with such an erotic accessory.

Secondly, in the middle of the 1980s, one could observe a revival of the idea of the wood gasifier powering vehicles. This idea was not new but long forgotten since oil was produced in sufficient quantities in the world. But the GDR had to import most of it and so welcomed the idea of the wood gasifier. This was installed in trucks, even by some owners of privately-run cars, but before it came to be used more generally, the East German State said good-bye to the world. Some people, not this author, in the final years saw the end coming, particularly since so many people were leaving, some illegally, more by means of an exit permit, the latter helping the government to get rid of their old-age pensioners and so to save a lot of money. But nothing really helped, neither tights for V-belts nor wood gasifiers.

In the end the following was a popular joke, which even comrades of the Communist Party *SED* told each other: One evening Erich Honecker, state and party leader, is coming back from an official trip abroad. Driving from the airport to the center of Berlin he is surprised to see that all streets are lit but deserted. He passes a hole in the Wall and discovers a note: Erich, you are the last one. Switch off the lights.

5 MEETING THE POLITBURO

Usually I started work as a lecturer of English at the Technical College in Merseburg rather early, at 8 a.m. On Thursdays my seminars began later, so one Thursday I arrived around 9 o'clock. When I had reached the third floor of the building housing the foreign language department, a burly man stopped me on the landing. What he lacked in height he made up for with broad shoulders and a thick neck. I asked him what was the matter. He said you cannot enter this floor. I asked why. He repeated in a louder voice that I could not enter, giving no reason. I looked over his shoulder and saw other men scattered along the corridor and looking in our direction, obviously alerted by our noisy dispute.

When I insisted, I had to go to my place of work, the man grabbed my waistband, twisted it, stamped hard on my right foot, turned me round and shoved me back to where I had come from. I limped down the stairs and outside met some of my colleagues, who stood there rather perplexed. All of a sudden, the department party secretary rushed up to us and said not to worry. Hermann Axen, member of the Politburo of the Central Committee of the Socialist Unity Party, *SED*, the Communist Party, was visiting the Institute of Socialist Economic Management, which was housed on the top floor of the building. And as long as Hermann Axen was in there, nobody was permitted to enter the floors below the institute. After having waited for about an hour, the door of the building opened, men came out and formed a kind of two-row cordon. At the same time a patrol car and two black Volvos arrived, windows of the latter curtained, and stopped in front of the door. A small, fat man, accompanied by three comrades, two of them carrying briefcases, appeared, waved at us and got into the car. So quite unexpectedly, though nobody had summoned us, we had the honor of being waved at by one of the members of the supreme policy-making body of the country, the Politburo, short for Political Bureau. I did not wave back, angry at what had been done to my foot, though two or three of our group of about 10 people did perform a kind of timid arm movement. The men of Axen's protection detail clambered into the cars and drove off with their master.

Who was Hermann Axen? Some among us, a few, said he was one of the thugs, albeit a fat one, of the Politburo. This man had the honor of having a joke circulated about him: A boy lies on the beach. Axen comes, undresses and gets into the water. Suddenly he yells for help. The boy jumps in and saves him. Axen thanks him warmly and says: Because you saved my life, you are entitled to make a wish, say what you want and I will give it to you. The boy says sheepishly: A state funeral. But boy, you are so young, you need not think of dying. The boy says: When I get home and tell my dad whom I have saved, he will kill me.

Hermann Axen, 1916-1992, was the son of Jewish petty bourgois parents. His elder brother Rolf was beaten to death in a Gestapo prison in Dresden in 1933. His parents were murdered by the Nazis about 1940 in the ghetto of Lemberg (now Lwiw in the Ukraine). In 1935 Axen was sentenced to

3 years imprisonment because of conspiracy for high treason. After his release he was deported to Poland because he was able to convince the Gestapo that he was Polish. He later managed to get to Paris and was untiring in his fight against the Nazis. The Vichy French arrested him and together with other Jewish communists delivered him to the Gestapo in 1942. Until 1945 he was imprisoned first in Auschwitz concentration camp and then in Buchenwald camp near Weimar, where he was freed by the Americans. He quickly made a career in the Communist Party in East Germany, became one of the architects of the country's foreign policy, was known for his knowledge of foreign languages (which distinguished him from most of his comrades in the higher Party circles), and was a member of the Politburo from 1963 to 1989.

My account is so detailed because Hermann Axen's biography is typical for quite a number of the leading communists in East Germany.

Take the year of the Lord 1986. The Politburo had 22 members, of whom 10 had either fled Germany when the Nazis came to power, deserted to the Soviet Army in the Second World War, fought for the Spanish Republic against the Franco insurgents, were imprisoned in penitentiaries or held captive in concentration camps having been accused of high treason, served in penal battalions or conspired against the Nazis when in the army. So, no wonder that we, particularly when we had spent our childhood and youth in the GDR, in the face of such life stories were inclined to give them a measure of trust and, because of their sufferings were inclined to overlook the fact that they were not necessarily upright humanists. For example, Erich Mielke, long-term Minister for State Security and member of the Politburo, had as a young man shot to death two policemen in Berlin and had fled to the Soviet Union to escape punishment; for this, and not for his anti-human activities as head of the security and political police in East Germany, he was sentenced to 6 years imprisonment after the German reunification. He was released early due to ill health, and died in a Berlin nursing home in 2000. It must be added that he took part in the Spanish Civil War on the side of the republic. He served in its political police, SIM, from 1936 to 1939. His main field of work was the fight against anti-Stalinist people among the republican forces and officials. Walter Janka, a fellow German communist and company commander in the International Brigade said in an interview in 1991, 'While I was fighting at the front, shooting at the Fascists, Mielke served in the rear, shooting Trotskyites and Anarchists."

As the top security officer of East Germany, he never rid himself of his Stalinist convictions and methods. In a 1982 speech before a group of senior Stasi officers, he said: "We are not immune from villains among us. If I knew of any, they wouldn't live past tomorrow. Short shrift. It's because I'm a humanist that I'm of this view ... All this blithering over to execute or not to execute, for the death penalty or against all rot, Comrades. Execute! And, when necessary, without a court sentence."

Our forgiving attitude, nourished by ignorance, was strengthened by the early history of the Federal Republic of

Germany, West Germany. SS-generals, *Wehrmacht* officers, Gestapo agents, almost the complete judiciary personnel, captains of industry, former Nazi secret servicemen, civil servants and others continued in official life and work even though twelve of the worst were hanged in Nuremberg in 1946. Some served short sentences in prisons, but most enjoyed good pensions and a quiet retirement. This development was partly due to the Cold War after 1945, when the Western allies needed West Germany's quickly rising economic strength and the anticommunist experience of old Nazis against the Soviet-led bloc.

I will here mention Hans Globke, Konrad Adenauer's Under-Secretary of State and Chief of Staff from 1953 to 1963. Under Hitler he was involved in drafting legislation on the confiscation of Jewish property, the removal of their political rights, and wrote commentaries on the Nuremberg Laws including the infamous law on the Protection of German Blood and German Honor. In West Germany as Chief of Staff he was responsible for the running of the Chancellery, recommending the people who were appointed to roles in the government, coordinating the government's work, for the establishment and oversight of the West German intelligence services and for all matters of national security. He was the German government's main liaison with NATO and other western intelligence services, especially the CIA. It is not surprising that under his protective hand old Nazis flourished in many parts of the West German society.

In East Germany beside Hermann Axen in the Politburo there were a number of leading political and cultural figures of Jewish ancestry who had suffered before 1945. To name but a few: Markus Wolf, chief of the *Hauptverwaltung Aufklärung,* managed the Ministry for State Security's (*Stasi*) foreign intelligence for more than three decades and penetrated the West German armed forces, intelligence services and political parties. Though observers agree that Wolf was one of the greatest spymasters of all time, in the end it did not help his regime. Others were Jürgen Kuczynski, leading economist, who could not become Minister of Economics because of his Jewish parents, Anna Seghers, most famous among the East German writers, Ernst Bloch, leading philosopher, Stefan Heym, outstanding writer, Klaus Gysi and Alexander Abusch, Ministers of Culture.

They all did not want to or could not speak out against the anti-Jewish propaganda present in the GDR for fear of being branded imperialist spies and supporters of the allegedly American-inspired state of Israel (though at the beginning supported by Stalin).

As late as 1984 the journal for children *"ABC-Zeitung"* published the fairy tale of the fire-dragon Zion, who lived near the country of the children of Palestine. The dragon was tiny and scrawny, could not spit fire, had a squeaky voice, was hungry and was on the whole miserable and poorly. The children of Palestine gave him to eat, but they did not have enough for the little dragon Zion. He became angry, flew into the fields, thrashed the ears of corn with his tail and ate up the whole crop. When the children broke into lamentations, he worked himself into a rage, became bilious green, could then spit fire and smoke and devastated the whole country.

The Politburo's membership was nominally elected by the Central Committee of the Communist Party, but in truth the Politburo was a self-perpetuating body that itself decided which new members would be admitted and which members expelled. They even decided who was to become member of the Central Committee, i. e. they determined who was to elect them to the Politburo. It is not unlike the Catholic church, where the Pope appoints the cardinals, who elect the Pope. The Politburo had power over the government, based on Article 1 of the 1968 Constitution: The German Democratic Republic is a socialist state of workers and peasants ... under the leadership of the working class and its Marxist-Leninist Party. With this unshakeable dogma behind themselves, the Politburo members could do a lot within their range of responsibility as long as they were in agreement with the General Secretary of the Central Committee of the Socialist Unity Party, also Chairman of the Politburo.

In the district of Halle, now essentially the southern part of the Land of Sachsen-Anhalt, Horst Sindermann was the First Secretary of the *SED* District Committee from 1963 to 1971. At that time our family lived not far from his house on the banks of the Saale river, which was a happy coincidence for my father. As a Lutheran minister he wanted to spend his retirement in West Germany, near one of my brothers, who had, by exit permit, left the GDR in 1985. Old-age pensioners were often let go as, firstly, they were no longer of any use to the workforce, and secondly, the government could leave the payment of pensions to the West German state. But for some reason, unknown to us, the local authorities did not grant my father and his wife permission to join their eldest son in Göttingen, West Germany. Finally, my brother wrote a letter to Horst Sindermann, who was at that time President of the *Volkskammer*, the GDR Parliament, and deputy chairman of the State Council, which were more or less merely ceremonial functions, but more importantly he was a member of the Politburo. My brother reminded him of their close local neighborhood connection and of the age of our father, then over 80 years old, and that there were no tangible reasons for not letting him move away.

Horst Sindermann, (*Du Blinder Mann*—you blind man— as he was called in one of the songs of Wolf Biermann, the famous dissident, singer, poet and song-writer), was one of the ruling communists whom one was inclined to excuse for many things because of his past. His brother was murdered by the Gestapo at the end of the war. Sindermann had spent 10 years of his life, from 1935 to 1945, in concentration camps. In 1945 he had escaped from Mauthausen concentration camp and had half carried one of his comrades with him, himself being emaciated down to a skeleton. He soon became a leading figure in the *SED,* and in the 1950s he was Secretary of *Agitation* and *Propaganda* in the Central Committee. It was in this capacity that he invited the writer Stefan Heym, who wrote a weekly column often pointing out deficiencies in the GDR in the *Berliner Zeitung* newspaper (*Offen gesagt*—freely spoken), to a weekly discussion of his column before publication so that they both could reach an agreement as to what was deemed acceptable to Party and people. Heym said that he could not live with this form of censorship, and as a consequence *Offen gesagt* was terminated. Heym, who had served in the US army and had sent an open letter to President Eisenhower protesting against the Korean war and had also returned his officer's commission together with the Bronze Star medal, concluded in his autobiography *Nachruf* (Obituary): "An established apparatus like the Party cannot allow to be openly told, every Sunday, how things should and could be done better. For Sindermann and his Party this was simply a question of survival."

Not a question of survival was the permission for my father to finally leave the GDR. We learned that Sindermann had notified the local authorities in Halle about his, Sindermann's approval, and you did not disobey a member of the Politburo. Fine with us. After the fall of the Wall Horst Sindermann, whose historical merit seems to have been having baptized the Wall "Antifascist Protection Rampart" (*Antifaschistischer Schutzwall*), was indicted for the "misuse of his privileges", but never brought to trial. He died in 1990.

Every Tuesday the semi-gods of the Politburo met in the building of the Central Committee, before 1945 the Reichsbank and now housing part of the Foreign Office. Then they went to work running the country. But running the country only happened between Mondays and Fridays. On Fridays they left their offices and let themselves be driven to their secure housing zone *Waldsiedlung* Wandlitz (Forest Settlement), so called because of its location near the place Wandlitz, about 30 km (19 mi) north of Berlin. The settlement was well protected, though not immediately recognizable from the outside. There was a 5-kilometer outer ring, consisting of a wire-mesh fence that purported to surround a wildlife research area. An inner ring was formed by a two-meter high, green security wall, which could only be passed with special permits. The whole area with its four gates was watched by soldiers of the Guards Regiment "Feliks Dzierzynski" and officers of the Personal Protection Department. This largely secret settlement had been built mainly as a consequence of the Hungarian uprising in 1956, when First Secretary Ulbricht feared that the leading comrades were no longer safe in unruly Berlin. The nuclear shelter there could house 400 persons. A staff of more than 60 domestic servants, all of them employees of the Ministry of State Security, served the needs of the representatives of the working-class. The overall number of people employed there was 650. Because the comrades spent a long week-end in Wandlitz, during which time they did not want to be disturbed, it could happen that a nation-wide calamity like the winter of 1978/79 could not be dealt with immediately.

So when at the end of December 1978 the temperature dropped way below freezing point, in some places to minus 30 °C (minus 22 °F) and a historic amount of snow fell, mainly in the north, the disaster response of the army and in fact of the whole government apparatus was only set in force after the Politburo had returned to Berlin on the following Monday.

This kind of isolated life of the Politburo members contributed much to the dissatisfaction of the people with the

Party and the government and was to lead finally to the downfall of the whole socialist system.

Hermann Kant, president of East Germany's Writers Union, a *Stasi* informant and member of the Party's powerful Central Committee, provided, prudently after the end of the GDR, an example of how people in Berlin felt in the face of the omnipresent almightiness, not to say despotism of the *SED* Politburo. In his autobiography *Abspann* (Closing Credits) he describes how he one day stopped at the red traffic light on the crossroads formed by a main thoroughfare and the Politburo's four-lane city autobahn leading to their Wandlitz place. The red traffic lights in the middle of the rush hour forced hundreds of cars to wait at least twenty minutes in the heat of a summer day for the black Volvos (or were they Citroens) of the leading comrades to pass. Next to Kant, in the neighboring lane, the driver mimicked a man with a rifle, aiming at the black cars. Kant looked around and saw other drivers grin. He said he could understand them, but then realized that he probably belonged to the group those people wanted to see before their gun barrels. At another time when he had to wait at the stoplights again, it was just two empty cars being driven past, probably to pick up their masters at their workplaces.

Over the forty years that the GDR existed the country and the people had grown accustomed to life in a quasi-dictatorship. Most enjoyed the safety of secure jobs, the health and welfare system, good schools, free university education, low rents (though often in very run-down flats), weekends in their gardens or dachas grilling sausages and drinking beer, and did therefore, grumblingly, tolerate restriction of travel, censored media, omnipresent secret police with their informants, shortage of goods and a polluted environment. Yet in the end, the desire for a bit more freedom, a better car to be bought without a long waiting period and a good supply of bananas became too overwhelming. Still, many resented the shameful way the State ended, which was symbolized by the way the last boss of the Party, Erich Honecker, was treated by his own comrades, who for almost 20 years had been licking his boots. After he was ousted from his job and finally from the Party, he was left homeless, being forced out of Wandlitz with his other comrades. Though many Party functionaries all over the country had houses, bungalows and hunting lodges, nobody was prepared to give shelter to the Honecker couple. Finally, a Lutheran pastor offered them a home in his vicarage, though Honecker's wife Margot as Minister of Education had prevented his children from attending high school.

Honecker and his comrades believed that they could make people happy by forcing their ideology upon them. For this they used the traditional instruments of power employed by communist countries, which were the secret police and their informers, the army, and the so-called Combat Groups of the Working Class (*Kampfgruppen der Arbeiterklasse)* together with a judiciary completely under the control of the Communist Party *(SED)*.

In the end they failed because the system did not allow for any adaptation to economic, political, social and personal changes in their own country and in the world.

Heymann's had the best beer in Halle, the good city on the Saale river. When asked why this was so Heymann said because it never stopped pumping, and so the pipes leading from the beer cellar to the taps on the bar were always clean. Heymann was an uncle to the West German Foreign Secretary Hans-Dietrich Genscher (who was born in a suburb of Halle in 1927), which earned him our deep respect and made him an authority on all questions related to foreign policy and inner-German relations and of course on the quality of beer. Heymann's was also the favorite pub of a number of musicians of the Halle Theater, which housed the Handel Festival Orchestra. Since my brother-in-law played the double bass in that orchestra and liked beer as much as I did, we were respected patrons of Heymann's.

Although we knew that he got his beer from the same brewery in Halle as most other pubs, we believed him. Normally that beer, having been made of hops and barley of low quality and enriched by a chemical stabilizing the froth, caused you headaches and could only be swallowed when washed down with Korn, a fine clear spirit made in the town of Nordhausen at the southern foot of the Harz Mountains. But everybody knows what a decisive role psychology plays in questions of taste. Everybody believed that Heymann's beer was the best, so it was the best. Another good thing about Heymann was that he did not believe in "last call, gentlemen". So, when midnight was approaching, he locked the door, switched off the lights, asked us, his faithful patrons, to sit in the back of the pub, put candles on the table, drew himself a beer and sat down with us and let us participate in his rich political wisdom.

When we all had our fill, which could be as early as 2 a.m., he took a candle, sneaked to the door, opened it and stuck his head through the gap. Then he usually sounded the all-clear, and we filed out and staggered home.

Adding to the safety of Heymann's was the fact that usually Manfred Jodschuweit was among us. He was the *Abschnittsbevollmächtigte* of the *Deutsche Volkspolizei*. For the moment I am leaving these two words in German since the first excellently mirrors the outstanding beauty of the German language and the second the power of the language, which can help to disguise political reality. *Abschnitts-bevollmächigter* was a police officer responsible for a definite neighborhood in residential areas in the German Democratic Republic, so perhaps neighborhood police officer would do for a translation. Literally it would be Section Deputy, but that makes less sense.

Secondly, *Deutsche Volkspolizei,* German People's Police, was quite the contrary of what the words say, it was neither *deutsch*, German, in so far as its power rested on the presence of more than 300,000 Soviet troops in East Germany, and it was not *Volk*, people, in so far as it was one of the main instruments of the Communist Party to maintain its rule over the people. That does not mean that the individual policemen were hated. Many of them, as the neighborhood police officers, often had their home next to yours, and their children were friends with your children. Also, they were often the addressees of minor complaints, mostly concerning security, drunks molesting people, traffic safety, broken street lamps that made people feel unsafe, noisy neighbors or bars and restaurants, parking offenders who blocked your car, vandalized waste bins, and the like.

One of our neighborhood police officer Lieutenant Manfred Jodschuweit's finest hours had occurred when the above-mentioned West German Foreign Secretary Hans-Dietrich Genscher got it in his head to visit his uncle Kurt Heymann in his native city of Halle. Police headquarters was notified and turned up with flashing blue lights in front of Heymann's. All the neighborhood officers of the district had been called up, and a sizeable number of plain-clothed *Stasi* (Ministry for State Security) agents mingled with the curious crowd that quickly gathered. The street cars running by the pub were stopped, cars held up and people on the sidewalks asked to stay back. A West German television team had got wind and rushed from Berlin to Halle to film this noteworthy event. The job of the *Stasi* was to prevent people from approaching Genscher and handing him petitions with appeals for help with their applications for exit permits. This had happened before when another well-known West German, the Bavarian Prime Minister Franz-Josef Strauss had been visiting in Dresden in 1983. It had been most embarrassing for Party and government when one could see and hear on West German TV how a poor beggar managed to get near Strauss and more or less shouted at him: "Herr Strauss, help me, please." He was quickly snatched away by the *Stasi,* though they had to be careful about what they did because at that time the GDR government was relying heavily on Strauss to arrange for a 1 billion Deutschmark loan that they urgently needed to show their credit standing to the international banks.

Anyway, when Manfred Jodschuweit had been employed to help cordon off Heymann's to facilitate the uncle-nephew meeting, no such unsocialist misdemeanor as in Dresden happened. And Jodschuweit prided himself with having helped to prevent it. We did not hold it against him because he was pretty hammered when he boasted thus and also told us about what he knew about the *Stasi*'s role in the event.

I was at that time living in a 19th century apartment house at the Hallmarkt, named so because it had been famous for its salt springs from which Halle (the name probably derived from Middle High German *hal* meaning salt spring) drew its importance as a salt exporting city in the Middle Ages.

Here is the place to confess that I am a great believer in law and order, particularly order. And as much as I disliked the GDR and its political system, I was inclined to appreciate the order imposed by the state on its citizens/inmates, and to a certain extent I helped to maintain that order in everyday life. That means I checked on people to sort their waste, tidied up the attic according to the fire protection regulations, and saw to it that people did their share in sweeping and washing the main staircase. (At that time, it was usual in East Germany that the tenants took turns in this kind of work, nowadays it is mostly done by a caretaker or a company.) And I also kept the sidewalk in front of the house clean. There were several old ladies living nearby who let their dogs, as if they wanted to spite me, crap in front of our house. At that time there was no law in the GDR against that. When something in the sewage system in the basement malfunctioned so that the floor was flooded with reeking waste water, I asked the hygiene inspection at the town administration to do something about that, and really, they sent somebody who replaced a broken valve and the problem was solved. But all this eagerness caused me problems. A few weeks after we moved in, the municipal housing administration, which was the legal house owner, sent a man who asked me could I please take over the voluntary, that is unpaid job of the *Hausvertrauensmann* or house representative, the old having died and been buried in the historic city cemetery consolingly named *Stadtgottesacker*, God's Municipal Acre. For this they would favorably consider our request to add to our flat two rooms that originally belonged to it but had so far been kept closed to us, the reason being they were reserved for possible subtenants. The job of the house representative was among other things to keep the *Hausbuch* or house book. This was a kind of logbook for the house and is a borrowed translation from the Russian *домовая книга, domowaja kniga,* where it was first used. After some pondering and talking to my wife I agreed.

This book or log was required by the GDR registration regulation and was kept by a tenant, usually the house representative. First of all, it contained the names, birthdates, occupations and the flats (for example second story on the right) of all tenants, including the children. If a tenant had visitors who stayed more than three days, they had to notify the housebook keeper and were entered into the book with name, date of birth, address of their permanent residence, name of the person they visited with, and the duration of the visit. Visitors from abroad had to be entered within 24 hours. They also had to provide the date of their entry into the GDR. Of course, the keeper of the house book had to keep his eyes open for any visitors the tenants might have and not report to the keeper. So, the job was part of the close monitoring of the people by the state. But I soon found out that you could evade being an accomplice to that. You just did not check on people, or you just did not enter the visitors in the house book. Once I was asked by the police if the residents really had so few visitors. I said I am sorry but obviously that was so.

The police, mostly in the person of the neighborhood police officer, the *Freiwilliger Helfer der Volkspolizei,* "Voluntary Auxiliary of the People's Police" (auxiliary police service), and of course the Ministry for State Security employees were entitled to inspect the house book at any time. But if you were not under any suspicion this rarely happened.

In my forty years—almost the whole lifetime of the German Democratic Republic—I survived with a reasonable state of mental health by making fun of them—them being bosses, politicians, administrators, judicial persons, police, *Stasi* and the like. So, in the case of the house book I started to get on the nerves of the local police department. If, for example, I had a visitor from inland, I entered him into the book as required, then went to the police and said that he was only going to stay for two days and 23 hours, so not quite three days. What was I to do? At first the duty sergeant showed some patience, telling me that the missing hour did not really matter, just enter the visitor. I said this was against the official registration regulation, could I please talk to his superior. He said okay, don't enter the visitor. I said can I still talk to his superior as just the one hour makes so little difference that I think the intention of the regulation, namely checking on visitors for reasons of state security, should be followed and the visitor entered into the book. The sergeant got red in the face, but kept himself in check and said could I please not make life difficult for him and do whatever I liked. I went away not without telling him that I might have another problem soon.

The next question did not concern the police desk sergeant, but the fire brigade and the town water supply department. It so happened that the General Secretary of the Communist Party, *SED*, and Chairman of the State Council, Erich Honecker, was to give a widely advertised speech on *Hallmarkt*, the square in front of our house. Days prior three plainclothes men rang our bell and asked to be shown to the attic from which one could look—or shoot, if one had a gun— at persons on the square. They inspected the attic, showed themselves satisfied and said they would keep the key until after the Honecker rally. Then we went down on the street, where a man was sealing the valve of the water pipe supplying our house. That meant the water would still be supplied, but you could not close the valve and thus shut the water off in case of a leak in the basement. I went home and wrote a letter to the fire department telling them that I could not in the following days enter our attic and get to the fire extinguisher and other materials like bucket, sand and fire hook placed there for fighting fires. What should I do? After two days a fireman, uniformed, came and wanted to have a look. I told him that the key had been taken by three men, who had not identified themselves. They had said it was because of Honecker. The man said he had to consult with his superiors. He came back next day and told me to rest assured that everything was in order. What, if a fire should break out, I asked? He somehow helplessly shrugged his shoulders, murmured something and went away.

Next, I sat down and wrote a letter to the urban water authority telling them about the sealed access to the valve, asking what I should do in case some water pipe broke in the basement. After two days a man came, looked at the sealed valve, then took me to the basement and showed me the main house valve with which I could close down the water supply if necessary. These are just a few examples of how I kept the authorities moving, having some fun at the same time. By the way, on the day of Honecker's speech on *Hallmarkt* workers from local factories, shop assistants, schoolchildren with their teachers and the whole city administration packed the square, there must have been some four thousand people.

Shortly before the end of Honecker's speech I had to collect our daughter from the kindergarten. I left the house and pushed through the people on the sidewalk to leave the square. At the edge of the crowd I was stopped by two policemen. You cannot leave before the end of the speech, they told me. I said that I had to fetch our daughter from the kindergarten, which was going to close in fifteen minutes. They still said I cannot leave. I got rude and began to talk louder, so before people around us became alerted they let me go.

Now I am coming back to Manfred Jodschuweit, our neighborhood police officer, who once came to my rescue. I had sold my Trabant car to a fellow musician of my brother-in-law nicknamed *Kaplan,* chaplain, because his hairdo looked like a tonsure. Of course, the selling price, as was usual, was the price for a new one, for which it was my turn, having waited 12 years. So, this was a great day for Kaplan, who got a car, albeit used, and for me, who got a brand-new one. We drove to Heymann's in what was now Kaplan's car and started drinking on a successful car day. Now Kaplan was a really great boozer, who hardly ever showed indications of drunkenness. After we felt we had had enough, we got in the Trabant to go home. Kaplan wanted to drop me at my flat and then go home himself. We happened into a traffic check, were stopped and asked to leave the car. The two police seemed to smell the alcohol and got really nasty when Kaplan began to shout at them, complaining about their stopping unnecessarily innocent people on their way home. Before things got out of hand, Manfred Jodschuweit appeared, who was commanding the traffic check. Obviously remembering the many fine hours at Heymann's, he told his troop to let go of us with the convincing argument that he knew us and that we were orderly people. We climbed back in the car and went peacefully home. Such things could happen in the police state GDR.

7 RUBBING OUT GEYER

Old Hugo Krieger, when he had reached his 60th, did not need to be told that he couldn't go on much longer as head of our department of foreign languages at the Merseburg Technical University. I didn't really feel sorry for him, even considering the difficulties he'd had in attaining his present position. He had been an *SA*-Storm Trooper and member of the Nazi party (National Socialist German Workers' Party) and an infantry sergeant (but as a teacher at a Wehrmacht school for interpreters not involved in any military actions) before 1945 beside his profession as a teacher of English and Geography.

About 95 percent of school teachers in Germany were members of the Nazi party (which counted 7.7 million members in 1943), otherwise they would have lost their jobs. As early as April 1933, two months after Hitler was handed power, the Civil Service Restoration Act, full name "Law to Re-establish the Civil Service" was passed, and if the German civil servants, which included almost all teachers, did not prove loyal to the new state they were to be dismissed. Civil servants who were not of Aryan descent were to retire. Our Hugo Krieger did not look very Aryan as defined by the Nazis, that means he was neither blond (and hadn't been when he was young) nor blue- or brown-eyed nor particularly tall. In fact, he measured about 5 feet, 7 inches (170 cm). After 1945, even before the German Democratic Republic (Communist East Germany) was founded in 1949, almost all the *NSDAP* teachers were thrown out and replaced by hastily trained new teachers, who had for the most part a working-class background and soon became members of the *SED* (communist party). In West Germany the allies also tried to get rid of the Nazi influence in the educational system and therefore encouraged academically educated outsiders to attend short teacher training courses to become teachers. But quite a number of the old teachers, even if they had a rather doubtful past, soon got their old jobs back. Not so in East Germany. Already in 1949 nearly 70 percent of all teaching positions were held by the newly trained teachers, of whom almost 50 percent were *SED* members, others belonged to the puppet parties controlled by the *SED*. So, the communists had a pretty good hold on the schools.

Krieger belonged to those who had got the sack after 1945 and had to find a new livelihood. He learned the trade of a mason and worked for a while as a foreman, as he told me, in a state-owned construction company. How he had managed to make a comeback in education he didn't let on. When I started at the foreign-language department in Merseburg he was already well-established as the department head. He had joined the Party and was a very ardent member who did not tolerate any deviations from the official socialist dogma. I could understand that because his past was well-known and he couldn't allow himself any political doubts, otherwise the college administration would simply have reminded him of his past. Thinking back, I believe that he did not like this precarious position too much and seemed somewhat relieved when he stepped down from his position. He went on working until his retirement as head of our English sub department, where he tried to keep us lecturers in check. We were eight colleagues, none of us member of the Party, and we stuck together closely.

A new department head was appointed, which we were to regret soon. He had the dubious name Otto Hagen, thus reminding us of the sinister Hagen of Tronje of the *Nibelungenlied*, The Song of the Nibelungs, who murdered hero Siegfried. I must admit that contrary to popular opinion I liked Hagen of Tronje because he was a faithful servant to his Burgundian kings, liked law and order, and uncouth Siegfried had not behaved very well when he entered the royal court at Worms. Also, he had cheated on Brunhild, when he helped king Gunter to win her as his wife.

Otto Hagen started his job by appointing two people his deputies who distinguished themselves by a particular ability to alienate almost all other staff members. Both of them were members of the Russian sub department and as linguists and language teachers of an astonishing stupidity. One of them was called a cunnilinguist behind his back, since he used to boast, when loaded, which often happened, of the many women he had had and what he did with them after the conquest. Naturally they were Party members.

A word about the structure of the foreign language department of the Technical University Leuna-Merseburg (German: *Technische Hochschule "Carl Schorlemmer" Leuna-Merseburg*) and about the ancient city of Merseburg. This technical university was an institution of tertiary education, the town being about 20 km south of Halle.

Merseburg lies on the left bank of the Saale river and was founded about AD 800 as a frontier fortress against the Slavs. It was a favorite residence of the German kings Henry I the Fowler, Otto I, and Henry II. It was the seat of a bishop from 968 until the Reformation and was chartered in 1188. Two more things are worth mentioning. Firstly, in the cathedral library are kept the Merseburg Charms or Incantations (*die Merseburger Zaubersprüche*), two medieval magic spells, written in Old High German. They are the only known examples of Germanic pagan belief preserved in the language and were recorded in the 10th century by a literate cleric, possibly in the abbey of Fulda on a blank page of a liturgical book, which later passed to the library at Merseburg. Secondly, the right hand, the oath hand of Rudolf, Duke of Swabia, anti-king to emperor Henry IV, of course nicely mummified, is kept in the cathedral. It was hacked off in his last battle against the emperor in 1080, taken to Merseburg together with Rudolf, who died a day later, and was buried minus his hand. He had won the battle, but lost his life and his oath hand, which was generally seen as a judgment of God, Rudolph having pledged loyalty with it to his lord the emperor. This divine judgment finally helped the emperor to secure his rule.

Part of university education in the German Democratic Republic was the obligatory instruction of the first- and second-year students in Russian and English as well as Marxism-Leninism and Physical Education. Therefore, the foreign language department, which also had a German section for foreign students, was a job provider for language teachers if you had the good fortune to be hired. In my case the story ran as follows. After graduating from Halle university as a teacher of English and German, I tried to get away from school teaching since I had found I didn't feel the call. This was not easy. There was a provision in the GDR ruling that teacher graduates had to at least work for two years at a general school before being allowed to look for another job. My attempt to avoid teaching led me to a doctor with whom my father was friends, who attested that I suffered from gastric ulcers due to a general nervous disposition, which would be exacerbated by the challenging work at a school. But the Ministry of Education, headed at that time by the strict and dogmatic Margot Honecker, wife of Erich Honecker, Secretary-General of the Communist Party and head of state, refused to accept the doctor's verdict and sent me to a secondary school in a small Thuringian town. This, by the way, proved to be godsend as I got to know my later wife there.

I spent two unhappy years at that school and then had another stroke of luck in that the municipal housing office could not give me an acceptable flat, and my headmaster was really well-meaning and persuaded the school inspector to let me go. I had heard from a friend already employed at Merseburg that there was a vacancy in the English department. Old Hugo Krieger personally came to Thuringia to have a look at me, had one of his rare lucid moments and recommended me to the Merseburg Technical University as a lecturer for English.

The foreign language department not only provided language instruction, but had also to do a bit of "scholarly work", to avoid the presumptuous term "research". So, the English staff decided to put together a computer-based English dictionary for chemical engineers, one of the fields of study at the University. This dictionary was a word list by frequency of occurrence and aimed at providing the students with words that were thus ordered. This would, we convinced ourselves, motivate the students to learn their technical vocabulary more eagerly. What we had to do was to find English chemical engineering texts, punch them into card machines, from where they were fed into the central computer in the University computer center, and let the computer count the words, arrange them according to their frequency of occurrence and print out the lists.

It has to be noted here that with regard to computer technology the GDR was lagging behind international standards. From these lists we composed a booklet, which was printed in the university printing shop in a first edition of 1000 copies. These were to be handed out to the students for a small fee to aid them in their studies. Of course, the colleagues who had contributed to this work were named in the imprint of the booklet. Now this is where Jochen Geyer, a new department member, comes in.

Jochen Geyer had joined our English department shortly after we got the new department head and was hated by the latter from the beginning. This, I think, had three reasons. Firstly, Beyer was on the point of acquiring his Ph.D. in linguistics with a thesis in the field of technical English. This is why he was able to help us greatly in our dictionary project. On the other hand, the new head of department had for years tried in vain to complete a doctoral thesis, in vain mainly because he preferred spending his time on women and drinking. So he envied Geyer his academic success. Also, Geyer was a really good-looking guy who didn't have to chase women, they chased him. One female staff particularly had her eye on Geyer, but our department head had his eye on her. She followed her good taste and struck up a liaison with Geyer, the second reason for Hagen to have it in for him. Thirdly, Geyer carried himself in a way that exuded a self-confidence that could even be taken for arrogance, which angered Hagen a lot. And Geyer didn't like being pushed around by his superior, followed his instructions only hesitatingly, refused to do more than a minimum of what was called political work and was at the same time an excellent teacher and ascending scholar with two or three publications in learned journals. But most of all the department head, as he confessed to me in a rare hour of intimacy—we had both had a few—was infuriated by Geyer's way of walking, a kind of strutting, which he had obviously assumed quite unconsciously.

So, from the beginning of Geyer's engagement, he was subjected to Hagen's petty hostilities. For example, there was the matter of the end-of-year bonus, which we were usually awarded and which in some cases reached the size of a monthly salary. Hagen leaned on Hugo Krieger, now our immediate boss, who had a decisive say in that and mostly succeeded in considerably lowering Geyer's bonus. Then there was the timetable. You could get your classes scheduled so that they were held either on three days or were distributed over 5 days so that you had to appear at work almost every weekday. Hagen got old Hugo to make the timetable as inconvenient for Geyer as possible. Then there were what were called civil defense exercises for the students, both girls and those among the boys who were unfit to serve in the army. They had to take part in a two-week civil-defense exercise at a kind of barracks, overseen by army officers and helpers drawn from the university staff. As often as he could, the department head delegated Geyer to these exercises.

No surprise that Geyer began to be alarmed.

One Monday at the beginning of the autumn term I made my way up the stairs to our department. I entered the office of the English staff, which was still empty. On my desk I found a note: Dear Christoph, sorry to have to tell you that I have left for good. You'll find all my stuff having to do with my work in my desk. Bye. Jochen.

For good! That could only mean one thing in the context of the early eighties. Lots of people left for good, most of them via Hungary crossing the frontier to Austria, which was not so heavily guarded as the frontier between the two Germanys or the Wall in Berlin. But whether you tried to get away via Hungary or tried to cross the border between East and West Germany (in danger of being shot or dying in the minefields), harsh sentences awaited you if you got caught. The Hungarian guards at the frontier to Austria were not so vigilant, and there were no mines or automatic guns, just barbed wire. Still, if you were caught, they delivered you to the GDR *Stasi*. People pretended to go on holiday in Hungary, which you could do without a visa, found themselves a local guide who knew how to get near the border and where the guards were and then left you to your fate.

Article 213 of the GDR Penal Code of 1979 made it quite clear that crossing the border without first obtaining government authorization would not be taken lightly:

"Anyone who illegally crosses the border of the German Democratic Republic or otherwise violates the regulations pertaining to temporary visits to the German Democratic Republic or transit through the German Democratic Republic will be punished with imprisonment of up to two years or be sentenced to probation, detention, or a fine.

Any citizen of the German Democratic Republic who in violation of the law does not return to the German Democratic Republic by the due date stated or who violates government guidelines for his stay abroad will likewise be punished.

In case of aggravating circumstances, the perpetrator will be punished with imprisonment from one to up to eight years. Aggravating circumstances exist when the act endangers people's lives or health; is committed while carrying weapons or using dangerous means or methods; is executed with particular intensity; occurs by means of falsification of documents, false notarization, or misuse of official documents or by using a hiding place; the act is committed in concert with others; the perpetrator has been sentenced for illegally crossing the border before.

Preparation and attempts are both punishable under the law."

I sat down and with considerable effort kept back tears. I had liked Geyer a lot and admired his resistance against Hagen. Now I felt a great loss. At this moment two things happened at the same time. The telephone rang and the door opened and Hagen came in. I picked up the telephone receiver and did not trust my ears. Geyer was at the other end, calling from the city of Flensburg in West Germany. I have often wondered why the communists allowed telephone calls from East to West and vice versa. It seems that it provided the *Stasi* with a good chance to monitor connections between East and West Germany closely.

Also, in many ways, especially economically, the GDR depended on the good will of the West German government, and it would probably have been, to say the least, detrimental to this good will. Cutting these connections would also have created heavy protests in both East and West. He said he wanted to talk to Hagen, department head, could I please put him through. I was absolutely dumbfounded and stammered: "Here he is", and handed the receiver to Hagen. I then left the room because I didn't want to witness what would probably follow. Years later after the fall of the Wall Geyer told me that he had only told Hagen what he thought of him, and what he could do with his job. When Hagen came out of the office, he was red in the face and told me that tomorrow there would be a plenary meeting of the 30 odd members of the staff. On the same day the Party group met and unanimously condemned Geyer's *Republikflucht* (desertion from the republic) and resolved to ask all colleagues, Party members or not, to distance themselves from the deserter. I had a good friend in the Party group, who warned me of what was coming. And also, that the main instigator was not the Party secretary, but the department head Hagen.

It so happened that I taught English to a group of three professors of chemistry, one of them having for some years been *Rektor*, university president. He was a scientist of international reputation and had good connections to the Party district headquarters. I told him about Geyer's flight and how Hagen was planning to handle the matter. That fiend had also told me that the name of Geyer had to be erased or rubbed out, whatever was the most convenient method of eliminating his name from the imprint of our little chemical engineering dictionary. This had just come from the university print shop, ready to be distributed among the students. The professor pulled some strings and Hagen got a call from the university Party secretary to call off the staff meeting that was planned for the next day. So, me secret prayer of "let this chalice of having to distance myself from Geyer pass me by" was heard.

But what couldn't be avoided was rubbing out Geyer's name. There was still too much of George Orwell's rewriting the past in the air.

Next day, the English staff met and set to work. As I was the first to make an appearance in our office, I was able to snatch one of the dictionaries, still unadulterated, and hide it in my desk. Then my colleagues arrived, then Hagen and Krieger, and we had a trial run. It turned out that using markers didn't work since if you held the page against the light the words "Jochen Geyer" could still be discerned. Some of us tried to paste the name over with a tiny square bit of paper, but here the same applied. Finally, we set to work with rubbers, which worked, only that you had to rub the paper very thin, so that one could see that there had been a name, now eliminated. I don't remember how many wasteful hours we spent on rubbing out Geyer, but I think it was the best part of two days. Of course, our seminars had to be cancelled, the rubbing being of highest political importance as Krieger repeatedly told us. The students of course were curious but did not learn the reason. One day later the security aide of the *Rektor,* who was in fact a *Stasi* (Ministry for State Security) man came and told us what we were to tell the students in case they asked why Geyer was no longer with us. "Tell them," he said, "that he had become *republikflüchtig,* that is had violated GDR laws and had thus set a bad example for our young people. His disappearance was not to be regretted."

A few years after the Wall had come down, I paid a visit to my beloved city of Halle. By chance I passed Otto Hagen, leaning against a kiosk with a row of empty beer bottles in front of him. He looked at me with glazed eyes not sure who I was. A former colleague of mine had told me that his wife had left him because she had got wind of his many escapades and was fed up with his drinking. Shit happens.

Jochen Geyer became a professor of linguistics at the university of Flensburg. Old Hugo Krieger died a few months before 1989, missing the chance of meeting old buddies in the Union of German Soldiers (V*erband deutscher Soldaten (VdS)),* which had as one of its aims the whitewashing of the Wehrmacht of crimes committed in the Second World War.

8 Living in a Socialist City

My god, were we happy when we were notified about our new flat in Halle-Neustadt, in 1965 called Chemical Workers' City of Halle-West. Flats were extremely difficult to qualify for, and many families lived apart and often in old apartments very much in need of repair. Most of those were heated by brown coal-fired old-fashioned tiled stoves, which gave the country its characteristic smell.

We were allocated a two-room flat on the second floor in a five-story block with bathroom, kitchen, small balcony, and, what was more than one could expect in the German Democratic Republic, a telephone. At that time only about 4 percent of all East German households had a telephone connection, and shortly before the end of the German Democratic Republic it had only risen to 6 percent. (At that time in West Germany the percentage was 90). We had to share our connection with another resident family, so it often happened that our line was engaged even when we weren't using it. This was called double connection.

After having been an English teacher at a High School in a small town in Thuringia for two years, I had in 1964 gotten a job as a lecturer of English at the Technical University at Merseburg, a town south of Halle on the Saale river. Merseburg was situated between the big chemical works of Leuna and Buna, one of the reasons why the Technical University was founded there in 1954. My eldest daughter was born in 1963 and was lovingly cared for by my parents-in-law 30 miles away in the small town of Zeitz, while my wife was working as a teacher of Russian in that town and living with her parents in their small three-room flat. I was the proud possessor of a motor-scooter which took me to Zeitz over the weekends. Not much of a family life, I would say.

But then the newly-founded Chemical Workers' City of Halle-West came into the picture. Though mainly intended to provide residences for the thousands of chemical workers of Leuna and Buna, many university staff of the Technical University Leuna-Merseburg were also given flats there. So, I wrote a petition to the *Rektor* (a quite famous professor of physical chemistry) and told him how happy I was to work for his socialist educational institution, which I could regrettably no longer do without a flat for my family, preferably in the Chemical Workers' City. At that time, you addressed a university rector in a letter as Your Magnificence, which of course I did, though I don't think that was the reason why he, a very decent and modest man, proved helpful. He might have felt sorry for us. He spoke to the right people using his influence as a member of the Halle *SED* (communist party) district administration, and we got the flat. Much later I taught English to a small circle of chemistry professors which included him, and he enlightened me about how he had done it, though at that time he hadn't known me personally. Needless to say, we never forgot his assistance.

The Chemical Workers' City, later Halle-Neustadt (I will use that name henceforth) was the offspring of the Party Secretary-General Walter Ulbricht's "Chemistry Program of the GDR", its history starting with a conference of the Central Committee of the *SED* in 1958, at which the settlement of labor in the vicinity of the chemical works Buna and Leuna was decided upon. They had the good sense to build the city at a great distance from the chemical plants, though when the winds were unfavorable, we occasionally smelled the carbide factory in Buna and could observe a grey-white veil on buildings and trees.

Almost all important political and economic decisions in East Germany originated with the Politburo of the *SED* and were unanimously passed by the *Volkskammer*, the East German parliament, and put into practice by the government and the respective ministries without any opposition or open discussion. There was, to be fair, one notable exception. The "Law Concerning the Interruption of Pregnancy" (commonly called abortion law because obviously few were able to understand how pregnancy could be interrupted and not terminated), passed in 1972 received 14 dissenting votes and 8 abstentions. Some Christian Democratic members didn't agree on grounds of conscience, which was tolerated by the *SED*. The law allowed women to decide up to the twelfth week of pregnancy whether to have an abortion or not.

The idea of adding new housing areas to Halle had been discussed since around 1900. It had a rapidly growing population and the north-south orientation of the old city— wedged between the Saale river in the west and railroad tracks and industrial areas in the east—was one of the main problems. Areas west of the old city and the Saale were considered. Because of the extremely difficult geological and hydrological conditions, especially a very high-water table and flooding from the Saale, the idea was discarded, but taken up again in the 1920s and then again shelved.

But true communists are not easily frightened off by realities of nature (nor are capitalists if they can get money out of it) and against warning voices they went forward with the plan. And indeed, from the start a series of pump wells along the eastern edge of the city have been in continuous operation, at a great cost, to keep the basements of the buildings dry. Levees were built or reinforced against flooding from the Saale, which nevertheless nearly set parts of the city under water in 2013, when the main dam could only be held with the greatest efforts and thousands of sandbags.

But at the time of our moving into the new flat this didn't concern us, mainly because they were only rumors and also because we were so happy having at last a home of our own.

All was well. In the mornings—my wife had in the meantime also gotten a job at the Technical University—we went by train on the newly built railway line to Merseburg along with the chemical workers, who, though many of them were afflicted by persistent coughs, smoked like mad. We, smokers at that time, too, could have done without cigarettes for all the smoke, but added to the nicotine haze by lighting up our own cigarettes.

Our second daughter was on the way and we again were fortunate: we were approved for a three-room flat in what was the longest block of flats in the whole of the country, popularly known as Block Ten. This was the residence of about 3000 people, a small town you could say, 380 meters long, 11 stories high, and housing a preschool and a nursing home. It had a roof garden (without any plants, just a tiled floor on the roof which we very seldom went up to) and as all blocks in Halle-Neustadt lots of green areas and little parks around it. The residents were encouraged to look after those green patches, weed and water them (with water from their flats, but that didn't matter as the water costs were included in the very cheap rent) and replant them, if necessary. I selected a tree and a few bushes in front of our block and persuaded my daughters to help me tend to them. They liked doing this and after a while were quite proud of "our garden".

Our residential complex had a health clinic, a restaurant, schools, kindergartens and a supermarket. Nearby was the really large Halle-Neustadt indoor swimming pool. All this was very convenient, and most people liked living in the socialist city. Later, interested people could organize themselves in "garage communities" and were given land at the edge of the city to build whole complexes of garages for their cars. Garages were considered real treasures by the car owners because most Eastern cars were prone to rusting relatively quickly. Also, the air was very polluted and soiled the cars in a short time.

I had a garage, too. We helped prepare the foundations and the green patches around it and then watched mobile cranes lift the pre-fabricated concrete garages in place. Of course, I had to walk in the mornings for about ten minutes to fetch my car but still was quite happy about it. As we had only a small flat and a small basement locker, the garage came in handy for storing a lot of other things beside the car, above all lots of spare parts, which one had to work hard to get hold of. In some places in East Germany where new housing was constructed garages were even connected to the central heating system, which added to the characteristic waste of energy of the socialist cities. You owned the garage but not the ground on which it stood. You could only sell it after the garage community had agreed. Every five years there were plenary meetings of all garage owners, at which a new chairman was elected or the old one confirmed. These for once were really democratic elections because everybody could stand for chairmanship. But hardly anybody wanted the position because of the unpaid work it involved.

I had a neighbor in this community who used (or misused) his garage for romantic purposes having prepared a comfortable bed in it out of camping equipment, a fact that his wife was of course unaware of. Whenever he parked his car in front of the garage, I knew that something lustful was going on inside. In all probability he was not the only one in the community to commit adultery in this way. Wives, mine included, hardly ever visited the garage complex.

Opposite our balcony there were blocks still under construction, and I often watched the construction workers on their jobs (I had at least one day without classes and could stay home). Regularly on Fridays they put down their tools and stopped their machines at about two o'clock, that means two hours before the regular end of their working day. Then it could happen that a Trabant car with a trailer drove onto the building site and workers quite unabashedly threw as many cement bags onto it as the trailer could hold and drove away. Nobody cared, though I wasn't the only one to observe this demonstration of *Kommunismus* where everything belongs to everybody.

Of course, they selected the undamaged bags, and those were not in the first layer of the pile. The first layer was exposed to weather and rain and got set and hardened, and was discarded. For people like us it was not easy to get hold of cement and other building materials (which you needed for building a dacha, for example), but as we were living in a workers' and peasants' state, the observation described did not strike me as too strange.

But another event did ignite a desire in me to protest and I reported it to the authorities. One morning our water taps didn't function, and looking down from the balcony I saw a stream of water coming out of a gap between two concrete slabs. So, there was our water running down the drain. Almost at the same time a water tanker came around the corner and stopped in front or our entrance. A loudspeaker announced that we should come down with buckets and other vessels to fetch water. I called my wife and we queued up behind the tanker and filled our buckets and a small tub and carried them to the lift in the building. I must admit that I liked situations like that. They had something adventurous about them, and also reminded me of my childhood in a small village, where due to damages to the central water supply during the war we sometimes got our water from the village pump. My wife didn't share such feelings. Hard to believe, the situation lasted three days, though myself and other residents worked the telephones furiously and told the local waterworks and the town hall what was happening. Of course, they knew already and said they would do what they could but at the moment didn't have free repair capacities. So, for three days we got our water from the water tanker, and didn't perish. Thousands of liters must have been wasted, but on the other hand in this one instance, because of the effort required, people were economical with its usage, which might have reduced the waste a bit.

Talking about water, I said above that the cost of water was included in the rent, which led to the most curious, and I must say unsocialist—or perhaps it was genuinely communist— behavior of the people. First of all, they weren't in any way thrifty with water but used it without a second thought about the costs. There were many who cooled their beer in the bath tubs under running water, and when they had a party, that special way of cooling could last for hours. They didn't want to waste space in their fridges, which again was understandable as they were as a rule small, just enough for keeping food cold. When I once talked to a Party functionary about this, he said that they didn't have enough water meters, and also that I should be glad to be able to use water freely, which people in capitalist countries surely were not able to do.

Did I say in the above that heating costs were also included in the rent? They were, but here it was the lack of heating control valves that prevented the maintenance of a reasonable temperature in the flat. There was just a kind of movable flap in the radiator casing above the heating element that was intended to at least reduce the ventilation and thus the waste of energy. But it didn't help much. I remember that from time to time we had to open the windows to cool the rooms down to a bearable temperature, thus heating the air outside. Sometimes in late spring or early fall, when it was still warm outside, the heating was on, so opening the windows didn't help much, you just had to cope. I once talked to a clever tinkerer who had constructed an ingenious air conditioning system. He had found an old ribbed radiator on a junk heap, connected it to his water tap by a rubber tube and let the water run for hours, sometimes days, to cool at least one of the bedrooms. He said the whole contraption did look a bit awkward what with the rubber tubing leading to and from the bedroom, but as his wife was pregnant at the time and was suffering from the heat, he believed he could lower the temperature by two or three degrees. He also said that maybe the effect on his wife was mostly psychological, because she could see how he cared for her in her pregnancy. It helped him in his marriage.

This leads me to the housing program, the General-Secretary Erich Honecker's favorite brainchild, which was decided—guess by whom? right, the Central Committee of the *SED* on its 10th plenary session in 1973. Three million concrete-slab apartment buildings were allegedly built from then until 1989, which made a lot of people grateful and reconciled them to their generally unloved country. Now imagine that what I said about the new flats and their heating and water applied to most of these three million units, you will come to understand what a huge waste of energy East

Germany was willing to tolerate. Added to this must be the fact that what is today called heat insulation was not used in the new blocks because it was expensive and would slow down the speed of construction, so that infrared pictures taken from planes showed extremely brilliant aerial views of the new socialist cities and quarters. This was known to many people—I knew about it myself—but couldn't be discussed in public as it meant the state had failed to develop a more reasonable approach to the housing program and thus an implicit criticism of the Party's housing policy.

The entire situation was once expressed with resignation by a government functionary: The poor man lives dearly.

My daughters attended preschool, kindergarten and music school free of charge or for just a minimal contribution for meals. Incidentally, when our second daughter was quite small, for some reason that I don't remember we gave her into the care of a very nice woman for a small fee for a few hours some weekdays. Her husband was a *Stasi* colonel, as we learned later, but was friendly enough when I once met him. But he looked like he could have been employed in the Moscow Lubyanka, the infamous headquarters of the KGB on Lubyanka Square in Moscow. I remember that I said to my wife I wouldn't like to be interrogated by him. Our daughter loved him and his wife, *Stasi* or not.

Kindergarten and preschool were important institutions in the socialist system. Women were meant to go out to work just as men. This was to be a sign of their emancipation (which didn't reach up to the higher echelons of Party and state) and was also important for the economy. East Germany was notoriously short of labor, not the least because there were hundreds of thousands employed by the Stasi and the police, as fulltime functionaries in the many political organizations and the widespread bureaucracy, and of course in the army. And it mustn't be forgotten that between 1945 and the installation of an almost impenetrable border in 1961 about three million people fled the country. An original populace of 19 million in East Germany at the end of the war had sunk to 16 million in 1988.

Also, by means of kindergartens the state could influence the education of its youngest citizens as early as possible. In 1989, 80 percent of toddlers had a place in preschool; in the large cities the percentage was almost a hundred. Places in kindergartens were provided for 94 percent of the children, while in West Germany the numbers were decisively lower. Preschools, kindergartens and after-school care were financed by the state with a negligible contribution for the meals. Clearly the majority of people welcomed such care by the state and could live with the accompanying attempts at early indoctrination of their children, because these attempts were futile. One of the reasons for the inefficiency of state propaganda was the growing gap between what the official media told the people and the reality of daily life; and of course, the almost omnipresent West German television.

In all fairness, one cannot reproach the East German rulers for not having tried harder to discourage the watching of imperialist TV, though they never actually forbade it in a legal sense (unlike under the Nazis, where you ended up in a concentration camp for listening to the BBC).

This all reached its climax in 1961 with the *Aktion Ochsenkopf*, when after the 13 August 1961 the Wall was erected. After fencing in the East Germans with barbed wire and concrete ramparts, the Party aimed at robbing their socialist sisters and brothers of the last still existing optical-acoustical contacts to the West.

Albert Norden, son of a rabbi who was murdered by the Nazis in the Theresienstadt concentration camp, was as member of the *SED* Politburo responsible for *Agitation und Progaganda*. His AgitProp department had developed a fine program, which was, not surprisingly, far away from political and social reality. On the 17 of September 1961 there were scheduled elections for district and local parliaments, and Norden's ingenious program was intended to be put into practice until that date.

The three-point program contained:

1. The removal of all television antennas, called *Ochsenköpfe* (oxen heads), suited to receive Western stations, summarily named after the second-highest mountain in the Fichtel Mountains in Bavaria, Ochsenkopf, equipped with a TV transmission tower specifically erected to broadcast into East Germany,

2. voluntary commitment of all TV electricians not to install "West antennas",

3. voluntary commitment of all housing communities (all families living in one residential building) to freely renounce the reception of TV programs from West Berlin or West Germany.

As there weren't enough *SED* functionaries to go around, the communist youth organization *FDJ*, Free German Youth, also called the "cadre reserve of the Party", was called upon to help Norden's program get moving. Young *FDJ* members, called *Jugendfreunde*, organized in groups and wearing red armbands showing them to be "helpers of the people's police" swarmed town and country and noted down all possessors of "West antennas". Then those culprits were asked, often by means of loud chants, to either turn their antennas in the right direction, that is away from the West, or else to disassemble those "opium devices" and "enemy flags".

In cases of particularly unreasonable elements the *Jugendfreunde* took down the antennas themselves and confiscated them; in some instances, although very few, they arrested the sinners and took them to the nearest police station, accusing them of having used hostile talk and swear words against the state (which they very probably had). This could easily lead to indictments of subversive propaganda and slander, which was one of the most malleable paragraphs in the GDR penal code. Addresses and names of offenders were published in local newspapers and the people denounced as spies and foreign agents. Questions such as the following, found in the Rostock *SED Ostsee-Zeitung* were asked: "Has not the time come that all citizens of the GDR get their spiritual input from the state in which they live?" And the Dresden *Sächsische Zeitung* postulated: "A decent German does not listen to or watch enemy programs, but turns away from them."

Even some years later, when the initial frenzy was over and the authorities had more or less resigned themselves to their subjects being disobedient with respect to Western TV, the attempts to at least discourage certain groups of people continued. In the army barracks and police quarters watching West TV was officially prohibited and could have disciplinary and criminal consequences. Those serving in the army and other military formations, and of course in the *Stasi,* should not even listen to or watch enemy stations at home, but who cared? This could hardly be controlled effectively. When it grew dark people turned their private antennas in the Western direction, and woe to the person who rang or visited their friends at 8 p.m., which was the time of the *Tagesschau,* the main Western news program. Nobody wanted to be disturbed at that time.

Everybody, including many communist hardliners (pretending that they had to learn what was really going on, which they could not from their own media), watched Western TV, and the Party had virtually given up fighting it. In 1973 Party Secretary-General Erich Honecker said, somewhat gloomily, that everybody in the GDR could watch and listen to the electronic media of the West at will. But up to the end it was not advisable to use information gained that way in public political discussions, and particularly schoolteachers were wary of doing that in their lessons. Though in the staff rooms they were less careful. Some clever minds used the phrase "I was informed that ..." and then a piece of information followed clearly gained from the West. But the phrase sounded somewhat sinister, and hardly anybody dared ask where the speaker had gained the information from. I, once, when asked about my source, said: Did you not read Secretary-General Erich Honecker on the 9th Plenary Session of the Central Committee saying ... And because nobody wanted to admit that they hadn't read *Neues Deutschland*, the central organ of the Party carefully, I got away with this.

We also had our private antenna on the balcony in Halle-Neustadt tuned to the west, but soon, I believe it was after Walter Ulbricht had to step down from his post and Erich Honecker became Secretary-General in 1971, it became quite usual for whole blocks and houses to have a quasi-legitimized central antenna on their roofs suitable for *Westempfang*, that is reception of Western TV programs. In rural areas people took the initiative and put up masts capable of *Westempfang* on nearby hills, connected them by cables to their houses and bingo they could watch the US Dallas series. People really internalized what they saw on Western TV, and it happened that they mistook the films for reality. I remember a day when I queued at the cash desk in our supermarket (called *Kaufhalle*—buying hall—in East Germany) and behind me an elderly lady turned to a friend beside her and said in a shocked and tearful voice: "Did you hear that Pam (Pamela Ewing) died?"

Every evening a mental or rather emotional "collective exit" of a large part of the GDR population took place, and for a while many people didn't live in the GDR any longer, but in an unreal TV world. Though ideologically this was alarming for the *SED,* in practice it had a stabilizing effect because people felt their deprivation of liberty as less painful. So a very astounding phenomenon could be observed (of which I of course learned only after the end of the GDR): The district of Dresden, where due to its geographical situation Western TV could only be received with difficulty (it was therefore popularly called "valley of the clueless") had the most applications for exit permits, and "political incidents", that is subversive language or actions, happened more often. Researchers tried to explain this phenomenon by the "collective exit" mentioned above which made people less hostile in the rest of East Germany. Or, as not only Dallas but also critical programs from the West were watched, people had fewer illusions about life in West Germany. Anyway, in 1988 the *SED* leadership quite seriously considered building relay stations near Dresden enabling Dresdeners to watch West TV. A crazier situation can hardly be imagined, because at the same time West media was constantly made responsible for most of the difficulties arising towards the end of the GDR.

A large block on the Eastern edge of the socialist city was reserved for the District Administration of the Ministry for State Security. To be honest, they had to watch over, control and hold in socialist discipline not only Halle-Neustadt, which had in the end about 90,000 residents, but the whole district of Halle with about 2 million people, including the unruly 50,000 chemical workers of the Leuna and Buna works. The caretaker of our last block, with the telling name of Fritz Sänger (singer) was an informer of the *Stasi,* and though he had been strictly forbidden to make this public, he, who liked beer and was really pissed at the time, hinted at it in connection with the following incident, which had to do with the actor, singer and author Manfred Krug and his *Stasi*-sabotaged concert in the socialist city of Halle-Neustadt.

In East Germany Manfred Krug (who died in 2016) was a superstar but in many ways also an unwilling subject of the *SED,* though often cast as a socialist hero in pro-GDR films. In 1976 the East German government prohibited Krug from working as an actor and singer because of his participation in protests against the stripping of citizenship and expulsion of the singer and poet Wolf Biermann. From then on, he was closely watched by the *Stasi*.

On the few occasions he was allowed to perform in public, one of which was the concert in Halle-Neustadt, he described them as a nightmare in his book *Abgehauen* (Scarpered). Our caretaker Fritz Sänger had been delegated to attend that concert. He told me that he and a lot of other *SED* members, *FDJ* functionaries and other people loyal to the party, about 200 in all, were provided with free tickets and instructed to sit silent and stone-faced throughout the performance. At the end, in particular, they were not to move a hand in applause. This they successfully did, and Krug describes the effect on him in his book: "It was the most hostile and icy evening of my life. They succeeded in letting me die on the open stage. Finally, I decided to close my eyes and sing, for me and the band alone as if I was in a rehearsal room. A macabre memory. Only stage people can imagine such fright and horror as I had to live through that night."

It is understandable that not much later Krug applied for an exit permit, which, after many difficult talks with Politburo member Werner Lambertz, the film director of *DEFA*, the culture minister and other influential people, was granted in 1977. He made, by the way, a successful career as a TV actor in West Germany after his departure.

One day a nice young man rang our bell and said he was the local Lutheran minister and asked if he could talk to me. I let him in, offered him a cup of coffee, which he gratefully accepted, and listened to what he had to say. It turned out that he was the minister of the small Halle-Neustadt parish that had as its center the old 18th century Passendorf village church (the village of Passendorf having been largely demolished to make way for the new city). Of course, there was no church tradition of any kind in Halle-Neustadt, and he had had to start from scratch to gather sheep for his flock.

The state, in fact the Central Committee of the Party, had from the start decreed that there were to be no new churches in socialist cities or new residential quarters, so the young minister was quite happy to have at least the Passendorf village church at his disposal, which the few church goers had helped to renovate. Though his parish was small, he was quite cheerful *in Christo, and* told me about the old vicarage in which he lived with his family. He then came to his point. Did I not want to join his small flock and renew my membership in the Evangelical-Lutheran Church in Germany, later called the Union of Evangelical Churches in the German Democratic Republic? We had a lively talk about religion, Christianity, Martin Luther's hate against Jews, witches and peasants and of course also the new social order in East Germany. In the end we agreed to disagree, and he left not without having expressed his hope that I might have second thoughts about rejoining, as he had divined that deep in my heart, I was still a Christian.

Living in Halle-Neustadt in low-rent flats, with good jobs in the chemical factories of Leuna and Buna, having a car, a telephone, a garage, easy and cheap access to health clinics and other social institutions, while the old city of Halle was in an inexorable process of decay, made a lot of people if not happy at least in many ways content with what they had. No wonder that in 1989 during the peaceful revolution and the final downfall of the communist regime most of the protesters came from the old city and not from Halle-Neustadt. The population, though often grumbling, had made their peace with the state.

9 MY ADVENTURES AS AN INTERPRETER

It is ironic that I, who was neither a member of the Party nor overenthusiastically committed to the principles of the GDR, was engaged to serve at times as an interpreter, whose job was not only translation but also the conveyance of a positive image of the GDR to English-speaking foreign guests, who, naturally, were from non-socialist countries.

How did it come about that folks like me were trusted with such a delicate task?

The answer is: there simply weren't enough people in the country who were at the same time ideologically pure and sufficiently able to speak English. When I was a student, out of the 12 in our first-year class at the English institute there was, as far as I remember, just one member of the Party. I wasn't what you would call a resistance fighter or openly anti-government—otherwise I wouldn't have been given the chance of university study. I was a fairly good student, got along well with other people, including foreigners, was most of the time cheerful and liked making jokes. And when my first job for the Peace Council (see below) had gone well and maybe those for whom I had interpreted had reported favorably about me to the trip organizers, the ball started rolling. It was only in the eighties that the *Stasi* began taking notice of me and created a file. But even then, I was allowed to teach English at various institutions like big chemical enterprises and the academy of sciences. It seems that the *Stasi* wasn't so efficient after all, because it took them almost three years to notify the said institutions about my exit application.

True, the *SED* communist party had in the end about 2.3 million members, which is a very high percentage measured by a population of 16.5 million. But among English teachers for example the percentage was extraordinarily low. Obviously, you couldn't be a lover of the English language and England and at the same time adhere to an utterly undemocratic state. So, the authorities had to be content with the people available.

My first job was for the GDR Peace Council, and involved a visit to East Germany by a kind of foreign dignitary. We were to meet him at the Central Airport Berlin-Schönefeld, but when we arrived, the first person we encountered was his German interpreter, who was crying uncontrollably.

One member of our little group led her to a bench nearby and tried to console her. The gentleman for whom she served as his interpreter seemed to have difficulty holding himself erect and was supported by a companion. The GDR Peace Council official introduced me to the gentleman and we shook hands. Then we went through the checkpoint, without being checked and through the gate on to the tarmac, from where a car took us to the plane, a Soviet Ilyushin IL-14.

What had happened?

A representative of the Egyptian Peace Committee, like the GDR Peace Council a member organization of the World Peace Council, had fallen ill during his visit to the German Democratic Republic, and the German doctors had found that he had terminal cancer and not long to live. Now the East

German government did not want him to die on their territory, which could cause diplomatic issues and problems. The man was a Muslim and therefore complicated Islamic rituals would have to be observed by his fellow-believers, who weren't readily available in East Berlin.

The GDR Peace Council was a political organization, whose goal according to the statutes of the World Peace Council, was pursuit of world peace, détente and peaceful coexistence between capitalist and socialist countries, disarmament, freedom, national independence, the abolition of neocolonialism, racism and anti-imperialist solidarity. But this was only on paper, because the GDR Peace Council was not part of an independent peace movement but entirely controlled by the communist *SED,* and therefore it never put in question the armament and aggressive policy of the Soviet Union or other countries of the Soviet bloc, and of course never criticized the apparent militarization of the East German society. The GDR Peace Council consisted of about 300 persons, among them *SED* functionaries, people from the so-called block parties, that is the other political parties in the GDR allowed and controlled by the *SED,* and also personalities from the churches and cultural life. A friend of mine and I were engaged from time to time to interpret for international guests.

At that time, in the middle of the sixties, East Germany was struggling for international recognition, which had so far been hindered by West Germany, regarding itself as the only legitimate representative of the German people. It more or less said that the Federal German government would regard it as an unfriendly act if other countries were to recognize the "German Democratic Republic" (East Germany) or maintain diplomatic relations with it—with the exception of the Soviet Union, of course.

The GDR tried to establish friendly relations particularly with third-world countries, providing them with all kinds of economic and military aid in order to encourage their diplomatic recognition of the GDR. One of those countries was Egypt under Gamal Abdel Nasser, and anything that would have disturbed this budding relationship was to be avoided. And certainly, the passing away of a well-known political figure like the Egyptian Peace Committee member on GDR soil was such a case. So, the East German government went so far as to make one of the government's airplanes available to send the visitor home, rather hurriedly.

Clearly the young lady interpreter was so overwhelmed that she was near a nervous breakdown and could no longer translate for the Egyptian. Thus, the Peace Council people had sent a car to my residence and had me brought to Berlin to fill in for her. My job, though I also felt sorry for the guest from Egypt, was easy in terms of language. I had to accompany him to his seat in the plane, ask for his wishes and translate the official words of farewell of the East Germans, who were in a hurry to exit the plane and see it depart. The big craft was then empty except for the crew, the gentleman's companion and myself. The Egyptian sat exhausted in his seat, told me to thank the lady again for her services and then added that he wasn't afraid of dying as he felt himself in the hands of Allah. He looked so sad and resigned that I had to swallow hard to maintain my composure. After I had said goodbye to him, the plane took off and we went all back to the terminal building. Here one of the Peace Council men told me in confidence that they believed there had been more than just translation between the interpreter and the Egyptian and that during the visit they had tried to terminate her services as quickly as possible. But the Egyptian had insisted she remain with him up to his departure, though, as we have seen, she couldn't hold out.

I was given some money and the railway ticket from Berlin to Halle-Neustadt and went home.

My first contacts with the GDR Peace Council as an interpreter had happened when I was still a student of English and German at Halle University. This was at the height of the Campaign for Nuclear Disarmament that advocated unilateral nuclear disarmament by the United Kingdom. It organized the Aldermaston marches (Aldermaston being the Atomic Weapons Research Establishment in Berkshire) from there to London (or was it vice versa?) and was at first quite successful. At the end of the 1963 march more than 100,000 people had gathered on Trafalgar Square. Songs were sung, banners swung, CND badges worn and distributed and hopes were strong that the British government could be forced to give up nuclear weapons.

One of the songwriters was Fred Dallas (later described by some as "the most vigorous, influential, and informed folk music journalists in Britain"), whose song "The Family of Man" became quite popular and even found its way into East German school textbooks. Fred and his wife Betty were invited by the GDR Peace Council to perform in the German Democratic Republic and I was asked to interpret for them. We went to various places in the GDR, such as Leipzig, Halle and Dresden, and Fred talked about the powerful movement in England with me as his translator.

As I was still young and inexperienced and my English vocabulary limited, misfortunes occurred. When the Dallas couple performed for students and staff at Halle University, among them my fellow students from the English institute, Fred talked about his visit to a cemetery of Soviet soldiers who had died in the fight against fascism. The atmosphere in the audience was respectful and duly sad, but then I, fool that I was, mixed up the word cemetery with sanatorium, and some people had to suppress their laughter. Fred had some difficulty re-establishing the solemn atmosphere, which he did only by intoning the famous American protest song "We shall overcome", which everybody joined in.

East Germany radio offered to record their songs, for which they were paid handsomely. So we lived quite comfortably in good hotels and had fine meals.

What is interesting is that during their concerts and talks in East Germany it never occurred to them to demand the abolition of Soviet atomic bombs. And when I asked them in private, Fred told me that the Soviet bombs helped keep peace while the English and American bombs served to maintain or achieve imperialist world domination. Somehow the truth was in between, I believe.

After they had returned to England I stayed in contact with Betty, who later became my eldest daughter's godmother.

After the Prague Spring and the invasion of Czechoslovakia by troops of the Warsaw Pact they reconsidered their communist attitude and left the Communist Party of Great Britain. In the end Fred Dallas, who later returned to his original first name Karl (his parents having named him after Karl Marx and Frederick Engels), even turned religious. He died in 2016. I don't know what became of Betty.

Obviously, the Peace Council and the GDR Miners' Trade Union had good contacts. So one day, luckily between university terms and shortly after my experiences with the peace singers from Great Britain, my bell rang and a delegation of two introduced themselves as representatives of the GDR Miners' Trade Union, Halle district branch, and asked me if I would like to help them with a delegation of Northumbrian miners, who had been invited by their brother organization in the GDR. And would I please hurry, because their car was waiting outside. I was a bit surprised but then realized that English was not widespread among the ruling class in East Germany, which meant they didn't know about the somewhat halting way in which I spoke English. I was single at the time. I was packed within an hour and off we went to Berlin-Schönefeld Central Airport, where we met three miners from Northumberland. Before we could shake hands and greet them properly, the ranking trade union official, who I later learned had never worked in a mine, underground or open pit, held up his hand to stop us and started his little prepared speech, which he read from a piece of paper: "Welcome, comrades, to the territory of the German

Democratic Republic, the first workers' and peasants' state in Germany."

The English colliers first glanced at each other and then around as if looking for the peasants mentioned. But then they took hold of themselves, shook hands and introduced themselves. It turned out that the two younger men, Alec and Jimmy, thirtyish, had out of respect elected the older man, roughly sixty, as their leader or president for the duration of their stay in the GDR. We, the Germans, henceforth called him the president. I will give him the name Norman. Norman had worked underground for so long that his way of thinking and arguing was somehow affected. And he spoke the most unintelligible Northumbrian dialect, which had not even gone through the Great Vowel Shift, meaning he pronounced the letter "i" in words like find, blind, pint or time as they are written like the "kind" in Kindergarten. This of course I could get used to and understand after a while, and "i" was the least of my concerns.

His mates had told me that their trade union branch back home had sent him on this trip as a kind of tribute to his lifelong devotion to the National Union of Mineworkers (NUM). And they asked me to take account of his somewhat reduced mental sharpness and try to modify his statements if necessary when I translated his words into German. And really, the first misunderstanding happened on our trip to the district of Halle, when Norman announced, without any relation to our momentary talk, that the reputation of the socialist states in the UK had suffered from the consequences of the "Cimmeton Pact". It took me some time to find out that he meant the Comecon, the Soviet-dominated Council for Mutual Economic Assistance. While I was trying to figure out that riddle, I heard one of the two German trade union officials say to the other that it obviously takes "our" interpreter quite a time to understand English people. I didn't justify myself but fumed, inwardly. Jimmy jumped in and explained what Norman really meant, namely the Hungarian uprising of 1956, which was crushed by Soviet tanks and in the aftermath of which Imre Nagy, the Hungarian Prime Minister, was hanged by his comrades.

The car trip to Halle was not without further incidents. First, I started to feel sick because I had served myself from Alec's strong cigarettes too lavishly, smoking one after the other, as by the way had Alec. We had to stop, I got out and threw up, which didn't help my reputation with the functionaries.

But then I was able to restore said reputation somewhat when we stopped at a motorway service station for coffee and a leak. Norman, being of a certain age, needed some time, so that I was sent to look for him. In the men's room I heard somebody knock at the door from inside of one of the toilet stalls. I called Norman's name and he more or less shrieked: "Chris, I am locked in!" Of course, I couldn't open the door from outside, therefore entered the neighboring stall, climbed over the partition and found out what was wrong. Norman, when trying to draw the bolt back, was pushing against the door and the bolt wouldn't move. He was almost in a panic, maybe as a result of his decades underground, where one can easily get a kind of phobia against being locked in, wherever that might happen. The others congratulated me on my noble rescue mission, and from then on Norman regarded me as his friend.

One of the requirements for official guests of the GDR was a visit to Buchenwald concentration camp memorial, which was a difficult matter for an interpreter.

Buchenwald concentration camp, 4.5 miles (7 km) northwest of Weimar was set up in 1939 and was one of the first and biggest concentration camps on German soil. Most inmates worked as slave laborers at nearby worksites in 12-hour shifts around the clock. Although there were no gas chambers, hundreds perished each month from disease, malnutrition, exhaustion, beatings and executions. Throughout its existence, some 240,000 prisoners from at least 30 countries were confined at Buchenwald. Some 45,000 people died at the camp.

Just prior to the arrival of American troops on April 11, 1945, the German guards and officers fled, and inmates took over. Later, after Soviet troops had taken over what was later to become the GDR, the camp served as Special Camp No. 2 of the NKVD. More than 7,000 people died here between 1945 and 1950. This of course was never mentioned to people visiting the memorial.

Though I had visited the *KZ* before I was still hardly able to look again at the horrible crimes the Nazis, the Germans, had committed there and elsewhere, and I felt ashamed when translating those details into English for foreign guests, though I had only been six years old at the end of the war. I always felt guilty because I was a member of that nation.

When we came to a big pile of children's shoes, hundreds of pairs of them, once on the little feet of children, murdered, I couldn't remember the right number the guide had mentioned and was corrected by our driver, who, as I learned later, was a *Stasi* employee and had some English. So, I had to repeat the right number, which made the situation even more unbearable. Thank heavens we had other experiences, which made me forget for a time the Buchenwald day.

We had to take part in a conference of the Miners' Trade Union, which was held, fittingly, in Karl-Marx-Stadt (today Chemnitz again), in Saxony. I remember that the chairman of the Union was present, an annoyingly pompous man, who gave an equally annoying boring speech about the upcoming elections of the shop stewards and their responsibility for the increase of labor productivity and things like labor safety and helping to put into practice the decisions of the communist Party, *SED*.

He really made life difficult for me, because he liked long sentences to which German is prone, particularly with the most significant part of the verb at the end, about which Mark Twain had already complained in his delightful text "The Awful German Language" from his 1880 book *A Tramp Abroad*.

Somehow, I managed. As it was mostly empty politspeak, I left out the most boring details, joked with my English guests, keeping a straight face so that the functionaries around me would think that I was hard at work. My British miners, being bored anyway, didn't mind and happily played along. In other situations, when a more literal translation was required, knowledge of Party propaganda and experience helped. You mostly knew what was going to be said because you knew what had to be said.

On our tour through the southern part of East Germany we went to Zwickau, an ancient mining city in the south of Saxony, where hard coal was still being mined underground at that time. The mines were closed in 1978 after having been in operation since the fourteenth century, first open pit, then, from the 16th century onward, underground.

We went down almost 3000 feet to visit the miners at the stall, who broke coal with their jackhammers under very hard conditions, hot dense air, low ceilings so that in some places you could only walk bent over, and dust was omnipresent. Here Jimmy, of our delegation, asked one of the German miners a very unwelcome question. To say the truth, I had instigated him to do that, knowing the British miners already enjoyed a five-day work week. Jimmy asked and I translated: How many days a week do you work? The German answered: Six. Jimmy said: We work five days a week. The German turned to the pit foreman who was accompanying us and said in his broadest Saxon: "Look, Willy, the bloody capitalists have better working conditions than we do." The foreman tried to wriggle out of this situation by mumbling something about every beginning being hard, even in socialism.

Of course, nobody told the British guests about the biggest mining accident in the short history of the German Democratic Republic, which had happened only a few years previously, in 1960, near Zwickau. Despite immediate rescue operations about 120 miners had died in a coal dust explosion at a depth of 3000 feet; only about 50 were saved. Though the authorities could not ascertain if any miners were still alive, they put up a wall in that part of the mine to contain the fire. I was careful or cowardly enough not to talk about this to the British. An offer of help by a West German rescue team from the Ruhr coal district with the most up-to-date equipment was rejected with the words: "We do not require such a hypocritical offer of help." It was the height of the cold war.

At the end of this visit everybody, myself included, got a very welcome bottle of *Bergmannsschnaps,* miner's schnapps, a kind of Orwellian victory gin, to make life look more cheerful. It was a clear, hard liquor, of which each miner got one liter per month for the ridiculously low price of 1,60 GDR marks, roughly the equivalent of a loaf of bread (today's price). Of course, this didn't help to reduce the widespread alcoholism among the miners. But their life expectancy was below average anyway.

That night, in our hotel, Norman, Alec, Jimmy and I met in Norman's, the president's, room and had a little party. Here Alec, a wiry man of medium height, swore to me that he would do anything during his stay in East Germany to get a leg over (a new expression to me which I immediately added to my vocabulary) a German girl, preferably blond and Teutonic-looking (his words), and then described to me in detail, fired by the *Bergmannsschnaps,* what he would do to and with her. I listened eagerly because, being rather inexperienced in that field of human activity, I wanted to learn how the English went about this kind of business. I assured him that I would do all to protect the German girls from his crude British imperialist desires. Norman, in his role of president, forbade us to talk about this delicate matter in such a way, then had a few himself and joined in. Jimmy, member of the Communist Party of Great Britain, being somewhat restrained and still unmarried, told me that he suspected I was critical of GDR socialism and politics, particularly as I had asked him to put that question about the working week in the GDR, which he now regretted to have asked.

During the whole trip we and the trade union people with us usually ate our supper in the best restaurants (GDR standard), and it often happened that fulltime functionaries from the local administrations of Party and trade union joined us with their wives to enjoy a free meal. I remember one little fat man and his wife in particular, who succeeded in doing that twice when we were at Halle. I had great difficulty suppressing a burst of laughter when he said to me that revolutionaries like himself must be prepared to sacrifice an evening like this for socialism. He was dead serious.

At the end of their visit my English charges and I concluded that we'd had a good time and promised to keep in touch, which we didn't.

Evidently, I had worked to the satisfaction of the Miners' Trade Union because a few months later, in the summer break, I was invited by the Cottbus district administration of the Miners' Union to accompany the chairman of the Kenya Quarry and Mine Workers Union. His name was Joseph. He was of Maasai descent, very tall and slim and black and kept saying to me that in this country "everything seems so scientific". I took this as a compliment and didn't do anything to discourage his admiration. For some ritual reason his lower incisors had been pulled out when he was young, so his English was not too easy to understand.

The Cottbus functionaries had hired a big car, I'm not quite sure but think it was a GAZ Chaika (Russian for seagull), from the pool of the *SED* Party's Cottbus district administration. Originally it had been used by some *SED* Politburo member in Berlin, but then taken out of service there and given to Cottbus. It could easily hold Joseph the Kenyan, the chauffeur, me and two union functionaries. One morning our driver came to the hotel after the appointed time with a big hole in the left front mudguard (he had run the car into a wall the night before on the way to his hotel), which couldn't be repaired in Cottbus as they had no spare mudguards for a rare Chaika. The officials didn't mind, but it led to Joseph's high regard for GDR "scientificism" being somewhat reduced. All the more so as on the next day the engine wouldn't start and we had to push the huge car into starting. That was a rare sight: In the center of the small town of Cottbus a black man from Africa, two rather overfed functionaries, recognizable by their Party badges and a somewhat plain young man who could be heard speaking encouraging words to the black man in a foreign language trying to start the car with the young chauffeur behind the wheel.

As if to compensate for this unscientific adventure we had a good time in an agricultural cooperative which for some unknown reason the chairman of the Kenya Quarry and Mine

Workers Union was to visit. I didn't see an immediate connection between mining and agriculture, but the union people obviously did, though they didn't explain it to me. Our good-natured African friend went along peacefully enough, we got an excellent and very substantial meal, washed down with *Radeberger Pilsner*, the best beer in East Germany, which earned Joseph's admiration. He confided to me that he was glad he was a Christian, not a Muslim, as many of his compatriots were, so he was allowed to drink beer. He had also for the first time tasted a sugar beet, quite unknown in Kenya, and expressed his approval. Only a very minor accident occurred that day. When we were led through the cooperative's pigsty, a big sow coughed through the grid and a large clot of phlegm landed on our guest's trouser leg. He was a bit taken aback (again fortunate that he was not a Muslim, God knows how he would have reacted to being coughed on by a pig), but soon recovered, after the pig master had removed the clot with a handful of straw.

Not really an accident, but quite an embarrassing situation developed when at the next stop on our trip we visited a miners' clinic, which the trade union was very proud of. They were quite boastful of the free GDR health service, but suddenly went quiet when Joseph, after having seen the dental department, asked if he might not have new incisors. Now this was naturally not in the budget of the miners' union for this trip and would have to be paid for by the union, because Joseph naturally was not covered by GDR social insurance. After some discussion between themselves the union comrades told me to explain to Joseph that regrettably we were near the end of his visit and there wasn't enough time for the whole procedure of fitting him with new teeth. He accepted that.

The trip concluded with a very nice boat ride on some canals in the Spreewald region, where Joseph was given a sample of the pickled Spreewald gherkins, which he seemed to like, at least he said so.

I had got to know and like him quite well, and when we said good-bye at the airport in Berlin-Schönefeld he, too, though scientifically let down a bit, was misty-eyed.

Working as an interpreter in the GDR (as probably elsewhere) could lead to some rather emotional responses. Laughter and tears were often quite close.

For quite a number of years the Ministry of Higher Education had established English summer courses for lecturers from universities and technical colleges. Native speakers from England, mostly left-wing or communist, were invited to help the GDR lecturers with their English and thus to make up for the lack of opportunities to visit England. During one of those courses we went to Freiberg Cathedral in Saxony with its famous Silbermann organ. The cathedral organist, who was tasked with explaining the organ to us, was a funny fellow. Though of middle age, he took great care to appear younger than his age, wore jeans and had a comb sticking out from his back pocket, as was the fashion among young people in those days. Also, he had carefully tried to make his sparse hair cover his head, in which he didn't quite succeed. So, he kept running his hand over his few strands of hair to keep them in place.

I was with the English tutor of our language group and translated for him. We both found this man very funny, and most of the time I was on the brink of laughter, when the following happened. The organist said that to keep up with his job he had to practice every morning on his big organ— in German there is the word *Orgel* for the instrument "organ." I faithfully rendered Orgel into organ, which my Englishman took in stride. But then the organist started to play, specifically showing his skill with the foot pedals, which caused my man from England to say: He likes a good foot job, too. I couldn't help laughing out loud, which made the organist stop, turn and ask me if I knew where I was and even said that should it happen again, he would stop talking and playing for us. This was one of the most embarrassing situations during my career as an interpreter, but I was saved by my English tutor. He said to the organist in English that he had told me a joke concerning organ playing and was sorry for the interruption. The organist had some English, understood the apology and was placated.

Afterwards Richard, the Englishman, felt it was his duty to make up for my embarrassment by telling me another organ-related joke, which shows how similarities between English and German words can make the job of an interpreter very difficult and render some things untranslatable: In an exhibition in the Bach museum in Eisenach visitors could see a big book with the caption underneath: Bach's Organ Works. A broadminded spirit had added: "So does mine."

10 Lifting the Iron Curtain

It was the straw that broke the camel's back. I was enraged and disappointed when leaving the office of the Pro-Rector for Social Sciences of the Merseburg Technical University, where I worked in the department for foreign languages as a lecturer of English. Though I had not really expected a favorable outcome from my talk with the Pro-Rector and my head of department, I had not come without hope. My standing in the department was not bad. I had in the past years successfully headed several English crash courses for scientists, executives, engineers and economists from the GDR chemical industry and the Ministry of Foreign Trade and was, though no member of the Party, head of the English sub department within the foreign language department.

My arguments were not bad, I had thought. I could no longer guarantee, I said, the required quality of my English without having visited a country where English was the native language, preferably Great Britain. The USA would also do, I told the addressees of my request, but more in an attempt to appear in good humor than seriously. How could I, was my argument, teach up-to-date English to people some of whom had been to the USA, England and other English-speaking countries without ever having been there myself? Was it not completely improbable that a teacher of English had during his whole professional life—not to mention the time of his university studies—not visited England? For good measure I added that it would not cost the University or the state a penny as my brother in Hanover in West Germany had promised to pay for the trip and the visit. Later I realized that it had been a mistake to mention my brother. How could they be sure that I would come back if I had such good connections in the West? On the other hand, I had wife and children in the GDR. Although it is true there were people who had remained in the west and then, after an agonizing time, had succeeded in getting their families to join them there.

Anyway, after the *Prorektor* and my head of department had talked for a while around the issue and tried to convince me that my English was good enough and that the political situation didn't allow them to support my request, I left. The point is that before going to the police to ask for a visa to visit western countries or just West Germany to see your relatives, you had to have the support of your place of work if this was in any way part of the state-owned sector or the educational system.

I had enough. I talked to my wife, who was also a lecturer at the foreign language department, and we decided that I give notice to the university, earn my living as a self-employed language teacher and translator and from that position, not being dependent on the good-will of any bosses, try to get permission to visit my mother in Hanover, who was at the time approaching 73 years of age. We agreed that, supposing I could visit, I would look around, see what things were really like in West Germany, which we only knew through talks with visiting friends and relatives and through West German TV, come back and then, if satisfied with my reconnaissance, would apply for an exit permit for me and the family, the pretended reason being what was called *Familienzusammen-führung*, family reunion. This was theoretically possible since the GDR had signed the Helsinki Final Act in 1975, in which the signatory states committed themselves, among other things, to respect human rights, to which belonged the right to live together with your family at a place of your choice.

Erich Honecker, General-Secretary of the Party and Chairman of the State Council, had maneuvered his country into a difficult situation. By signing the 1975 Act on an equal footing with West Germany's Federal Chancellor Helmut Schmidt he had earned himself the much-craved international recognition as a sovereign state in its own right, but had run into trouble in the interior. From now on GDR citizens could claim all sorts of human rights, including the choice of where to live. So, from then on, the number of applications for *Familienzusammenführung* grew steadily. People discovered relatives in the West with whom they had had hardly any contacts, but now urgently wanted to share their lives with. In our case I had my father and my mother, who had been divorced for decades, and two brothers in West Germany whom I could all, particularly my mother, claim to love beyond measure and without whom life for me and my family had simply become unbearable.

But first of all, as I said, I just wanted to visit. No longer needing any boss's permission, I applied for a visa and got one. My mother was born on September 12, 1913, so I applied for what was called a visitor's visa for her 73rd birthday, claiming that her being in poor health and not expecting to live much longer made my visit urgent. In fact, my mother went swimming every day and, God be thanked, lived to the blessed age of 96. My plan was to travel to Hanover and from there to England, though this would have been illegal. But it didn't work out like that. As soon as I arrived at my brother's, the new impressions were so overwhelming and our joy to be together in his world (he used to visit me every two or three years in my place in Halle) so great that we rather excessively celebrated the six days which my visa allowed. Of course, I saw my father and my mother and looked around as much as I could, but looking back from today I remember that week as mainly immersed in an alcoholic haze.

On one of my last days I had a serious and sober talk with my brother. We discussed the question of me staying in Hanover, trying to find a job and then doing everything I could to get my family to join me. But it did not take us long to decide that this would be out of the question. My wife would certainly lose her job, would be harassed by the *Stasi* as a possible accessory to a crime, namely *Republikflucht* (Escape from the Republic), would only make a very scarce living and generally become very miserable. And experience from friends had told us that it could take years before she would be allowed to follow me to the West, if at all.

I can hardly describe my feelings when I returned to Halle. It felt like going back to prison. When I handed in my passport at police headquarters, I remember I virtually threw it on their desk and left without a word. I suppose such a reaction was not unfamiliar to them. Now our decision was clear. We wanted to leave, hazarding the consequences.

Curiously enough we were confident of getting jobs in West Germany corresponding to our qualifications. My brother and his wife had promised to give us accommodation in their house until we would find a flat. That means we would not have to go to a refugee reception center as many people had to.

So now we set in motion the troublesome and dangerous process of applying for permanent exit from East to West Germany and the dismissal from the citizenship of the German Democratic Republic.

Officially this application was not legal, despite everything said and signed in the Helsinki Act. Or rather, nobody knew exactly if it was legal or not, you were intentionally kept in uncertainty and given the feeling that you could be in some ways held accountable any time.

The application for the permanent exit permit *(Ausreise-antrag)* was a popular term for what in GDR red tape was called relocation request *(Übersiedlungsersuchen)*. The applicants were usually regarded as "negative-hostile elements" and by many among the population regarded with enmity and also envy, a curious mixture. In the period between the construction of the Wall on August 13, 1961 and its fall on November 9, 1989 more than 500,000 people left East Germany by means of this relocation request. For a long time, they were for the most part old-age pensioners, whose emigration even helped the state to get rid of unproductive and therefore superfluous eaters, who had flats and got pensions all of which the state could make good use of. Later, particularly after the Helsinki Act of 1975, more and more young people tried their luck, outnumbering the elderly.

This seemingly legal, half-legal or even illegal way often entailed precarious consequences such as loss of job, reprisals against the whole family, being watched by the *Stasi* as well as criminal prosecution which could end up in prison sentences. Additionally, the permission to leave the country was in most cases granted only after permanent and persistent assertion of your wish, in oral and written form, at the relevant authorities, which were the Departments for Home Affairs.

Of course, those authorities closely cooperated with the Ministry of State Security, and you never knew if, or rather you could be pretty sure that the official was either a *Stasi* employee or an informant. The intention of this grueling process was obvious: the exit visa applicant, whom the state regarded as a public enemy, was to be physically and mentally worn down. The whole procedure could last between one and ten years.

The request was usually rejected several times, never in writing, and reasons were not given. The opposition groups and "Monday Demonstrations", often under the roof of the Protestant church, were to a large extent formed by the applicants mentioned. They developed a growing rage and were often ready to do what was regarded in the GDR as illegal like distributing anti-GDR pamphlets, often hand-written, or painting slogans on walls, by this risking prison sentences. A number sought refuge in churches, as there was a tacit agreement between church and state to let them leave the country if this could be done without much publicity. There happened a notable exception in Weimar. In December 1988 five men and women were so desperate that they locked themselves in the sacristy of the Herder Church to force their exit. The superintendent asked them to leave, and when they refused, he called the *Stasi* and they were arrested and imprisoned until September 1989. This superintendent, by the way, said in a private talk in 1988 that when he retired, he would immediately go to West Germany. This was the only known example of the church calling police or *Stasi* for help against would-be exit-seekers.

My wife and I were aware of all these consequences but determined to bear the hazards. So, after my return from Hanover and some weeks of deliberation and of course much trepidation we prepared a written application:

"Application for the permanent exit from the GDR to the BRD and the dismissal from the citizenship of the GDR

We herewith apply for permanent exit from the GDR to the BRD and the dismissal from the citizenship of the GDR.

Date and signatures"

We went to the Department for Home Affairs of our city district on October 8, 1986, and were seen by two officials, a man and a woman, who took our application and told us to wait and do nothing in the way of public protests or taking part in any subversive activities as this would only prove detrimental to our request. They were not completely unfriendly, just factual, and gave us the impression without saying it in so many words that the quieter we went on living the more favorably our application would be handled. And we believed them, which was a big mistake.

Next day my wife came home from work early, and after entering the flat immediately started to cry (though we knew what was to be expected). In the middle of one of her English lessons to students of chemical engineering at Merseburg Technical University her department head interrupted her teaching and told her to come out. Quick *Stasi* work, one must admit. He told her to tell the students that she had some urgent business, therefore had to end the class and would see them the following week. Outside the room her boss told her that he had been informed that she had applied for a permanent exit visa, therefore could no longer teach students in a socialist educational institution. He watched her taking her personal belongings from her desk and leave the campus. Now even in the GDR you could not simply be fired without being given a reason. As they had no real one except that she was all of a sudden regarded unfit to teach, they offered her a job as a cleaning woman at the university, obviously sure that she would never accept it. And now we made our biggest mistake. Instead of *Frau Doktor* accepting the offer and going about the university with a broom, a bucket and a floor cloth, which would certainly have caused a scandal among staff and students and therefore with high probability accelerated our exit, we did not want to provoke and anger the authorities and therefore my wife gave notice. Moreover, in a final talk, the university personnel officer (called *Kaderleiter* at that time) lied to us as had the two people at the Department for Home Affairs saying that we would be wise not to do anything provocative at the university or elsewhere in order not to impair our application. With hindsight I must say they would certainly not have her let go about as a cleaning woman as they could not have been that stupid not to foresee a scandal.

From now on for the next three years we depended financially on what I earned as a free-lancer, which was more than enough. I did technical translations for *Intertext*, the GDR central foreign language service, and held English courses mainly at three institutions, which were the Leuna Works, at that time the biggest chemical factory with about 30,000 employees, the ORWO Film Factory Wolfen and the Academy of Sciences at Leipzig. I am still wondering today that the *Stasi* did not find out about these courses or just did not look closely enough. Only three years after we had first handed in our application, in 1989, did the three institutions inform me that they could not prolong my contract, the reason given was the unclear term "restructuring", obviously a pretext; one nice woman in Wolfen told me the real reason, which was my exit application. Did the *Stasi* administration in the various places not communicate with each other properly? I was certainly merely a minor figure, but the institutions mentioned were not minor. And in my courses sat the usual informers, as I could see from my *Stasi* files after 1989. They had faithfully sent their reports to their controllers or case officers. All of them wrote in their memos that Werner in his lessons showed a "negative-hostile" attitude towards our socialist state. Now mind you, all I usually did when I started a course was to make the observation that the united efforts of Party and State had prevented me from spending some time in England. So, they had to be satisfied with what I offered them in the way of modern English. Oh, and also from time to time I talked about what a literal translation of foreign words into plain German would produce. General-Secretary would thus yield general secret scribe (*allgemeiner Geheimschreiber)* and *Agitation* and *Propaganda,* one of the most important activities of the Party propagandists, could just be interpreted as unrest and dissemination. I knew what I was doing, but just thought that life would be easier for me and the course members if we had some fun.

Other things were also reported, as I could see from my file. I usually underlined the importance of learning foreign languages by two examples. The biggest East German pharmaceutical enterprise was GERMED (for GERman MEDicine) in Dresden. I told the courses that it was not a good idea for a firm exporting medicaments to call themselves germed, which meant among other things full of bacteria, germs. And it was also not good for the *Schwer-maschinenbau-Kombinat "Ernst Thälmann"* in Magdeburg (heavy engineering works) to use the abbreviation SKET, which could easily be taken for skit, the Swedish word for shit, Sweden being an importer of the products of SKET. This was all the worse as Ernst Thälmann was a highly honored communist leader, who was killed by the Nazis in Buchenwald concentration camp.

I am still convinced that these examples served their purpose, namely stressing that learning foreign languages was a much-needed requirement. Maybe I made a bit of fun of those responsible for these language blunders, and the *Stasi* informers therefore took them as "negative-hostile".

But obviously they did not have at that time a functioning exchange of information by means of, for example, a central data base, otherwise they would have found out earlier that the freelance language teacher and the exit visa applicant were one and the same person. They also got other things wrong like our home address, at least for a time, and my sister-in-law in Hanover, whom they believed to be my sister. Later I came more and more to believe that one of the *Stasi*'s main instruments of control were not so much their comprehensive surveillance programs, though they tried their best, but their success in making people believe in their omnipotence and thus intimidate them.

Anyway, for the first year after we had started our exit application process, we followed my misguided strategy of keeping quiet, wrongly believing that would help us. And we were constantly told by the relevant department that this was the right thing to do and would be favorably regarded.

But realizing with time that we weren't making any progress and learning of applicants who had started their requests later than we but were leaving earlier, having protested publicly and gotten on the nerves of the authorities, we began anew. We wrote a new application with a detailed justification, mainly concentrating on the need to be together with my parents in the West, who were getting on in age. This application I sent to Honecker, General-Secretary of the Party and head of state, to the district Party secretary and member of the Politburo, the Halle district attorney (to whom we complained that Honecker had not answered our petition, which he should have done according to the "Law concerning petitions" in the GDR, which ruled that petitions to government agencies and similar organizations had to be answered within four weeks), to the Ministry for State Security (complaining that I had been wrongly accused of having taken part in a demonstration on the market place in Halle), to the President of the *Volkskammer* (East German Parliament), to the mayor of Halle and to the district police headquarters. At the same time my brother and my mother wrote to the mayor in Hanover, to Federal Chancellor Kohl, the Foreign Secretary Genscher in Bonn and to a lawyer in Westberlin who acted for the West German Government in cases such as ours. All the West German agencies reacted and promised to help.

The Halle district attorney invited us for a talk, of which I found the following document in my file. It should be remembered that at that time GDR socialism had just one year more to live.

Halle, July 5, 1989
District Attorney's Office
Ja/Kl
Memo
The Werner couple, personal data known, appeared as summoned on June 13, 1989 from 10 to 10.45 a.m. and were received by Comrade *(Genossin)* Manncck.

Because of the provocative behavior of the couple an orderly dialogue was not possible. Dr. Werner was the spokesman, supported and supplemented by his wife.

Concerning the content of the talk Comrade Manneck states that no result was reached. From the beginning Dr. Werner said he would not accept oral answers. He demanded that his questions be answered in a written form, and if he did not get them, he would know where to turn to. Further he demanded to know to whom he could turn in the BRD (West Germany) without violating GDR laws.

Comrade Manneck answered that to involve persons, organizations and others in exit applications could have penal consequences. Thereupon Dr. Werner said he would turn to an international organization that campaigned against occupational bans, because such a ban had been imposed on him and his wife. He regretted that they themselves had given notice so that now they were not in a position to bring their occupational ban before a court.

His next steps, Dr. Werner announced, would be to write to district police headquarters, the Ministry of the Interior and to the Halle district council. They would also file a complaint with the county court. All this was to be undertaken to help their exit application.

Because an orderly dialogue was not possible, Comrade Manneck terminated the interview.

Date
Prosecutor

What Comrade Manneck referred to in her memo with regard to international organizations was the International Labor Organization, ILO, a United Nations Agency pursuing decent work and justice for workers. In 1969 the ILO had received the Nobel Peace Prize for its work. The German Democratic Republic since it had become a member of the UNO in 1973 was also member of the ILO. In fact I had asked the district attorney in a letter if I could turn to the ILO for help, because it was a member of the UNO, to which the GDR belonged, and thus such a request could hardly be regarded as "illegal liaising with a foreign state or organization", which was punishable under GDR law, as Comrade Manneck had pointed out.

As one can see from the memo, this question was not directly answered. § 219 of the GDR Penal Code read that punishable is "who (1) disseminates or lets disseminate information abroad which can be used to harm the interests of the GDR or who for this purpose produces or lets produce records, (2) who transfers or lets transfer manuscripts or printed material of any kind to organizations, institutions or persons in foreign countries, which can be used to harm the interests of the GDR, violating thereby the laws of the GDR".

It is clear that under such vague rules any connection with abroad could be punished.

Here follows a memo of the Ministry for State Security District Administration Halle following a complaint I had sent to that institution.

District Administration for State Security Halle
Investigation Department
Halle, July 10, 1989

Memo
on a further talk with WERNER, Christoph.

On July 10, 1989 at 10 to 10.30 a. m. another talk with Dr. WERNER took place in Department K *(Criminal Investigation Department)* of the BDVP *(District Police Headquarters)* Halle.

This was occasioned by the answer of the VPKA *(Local Police Headquarters)* Halle to a petition WERNER had sent on November 27, 1988.

The demand to Werner not to stop and stay on the market place in Halle on Mondays between 18 and 20 hours was lifted. *(this was the time of the Monday Demonstrations for more democracy in the GDR. People gathered in front of the Market Church, held candles in their hands and carried all kinds of signs and badges, not in the least subversive, like "swords to ploughshares").*

But Dr. WERNER was told again that the demand of June 30, 1989 remained fully valid. *(Obviously this was the demand not to take part in any demonstrations on the market place).*

He expressed that he would follow that request if it would help his exit application and that he would tell his wife so.

Signature (unreadable)

These were just two examples of the many running battles between us and the authorities, which almost wore us down, had it not been for the contacts with other applicants and the encouragement we gave each other. And also, we did not lose hope that the efforts from the side of my brother in West Germany would bear fruit.

There were certain places in Halle or near it, where you could be sure to meet and talk to other applicants. And always word got around that so-and-so had left and that so-and-so would leave very soon. One of those places was an open-air swimming pool to the north of Halle near Petersberg, which we frequented in summer, and a garden restaurant in a suburb. The applicants meeting there talked freely about the progress they had made or not made despite the fact that everybody knew there were *Stasi* among the crowd.

Mostly we found ourselves in a somewhat eerie situation when we were among friends and acquaintances and people who had decided they would try their luck with "real-existing socialism" (an ideological catchphrase popularized during the Brezhnev era within the Eastern bloc countries and the Soviet Union. The term referred to the Soviet-type economic planning enforced by the ruling communist parties and was aimed at distinguishing them from Trotskyist, Maoist and Eurocommunist ideas. People made fun of the term: Armenian Radio was asked: "Is it possible to build real-existing socialism in Armenia?" Armenian Radio answers: "Yes, but rather in Georgia").

The application for the "Dismissal from the citizenship of the German Democratic Republic" made one a legal entity of a special kind. They no longer belonged to the "socialist community". They had broken from the community of the well-behaved, the modest and the conforming. Of course, they bore a heightened risk, but their behavior also contained something that was regarded by those who were remaining as outrageous and lacking solidarity. Most of the GDR-typical topics such as house-hunting, waiting time for the Trabant car or searching for spare parts were no longer matters of concern or only in a nostalgic kind of way. While others planned their next year's Baltic Sea holiday or discussed how to get building materials for their dachas, those who had applied to leave listened indifferently. They had become strangers in their own country, already feeling almost as visitors from the West. They didn't even worry any more about the political situation. They had capitulated and no longer believed in any political changes or improvements. The only thing they were interested in was finding ways to quicken their exit.

The state lived also in a kind of ambivalence. On the one hand it wanted to relieve the pressure in the interior by cautiously granting more exit visas. On the other hand, it felt compelled to apply repressive measures in order to remain master of the situation and control the exit movement. The softer it got, the more people applied for exit visas, the harsher it got, the more pressure was produced. This dilemma finally contributed to its downfall.

Despite all the protests, the unrest, the Monday Demonstrations, the many people who left for West

Germany, some of whom were shot and killed at the Wall, the implausibility of the official propaganda, the shortage of so many things, the old men in the Politburo who couldn't hold their water let alone make reasonable decisions, and despite the hopes that were fired by the appearance of the reformer Gorbachev as General-Secretary of the Soviet Communists we didn't believe any changes for the better were possible. This impression was strengthened by observations such as the following.

The *Marktplatz* (market place) in the city of Halle became more and more the center of demonstrations and rallies against the rule of the Party. Hundreds, sometimes thousands gathered peacefully and defied the police. On one such occasion, it must have been as late as the summer of 1989, the police, the paramilitary organization of the "Combat Groups of the Working-Class", the *Stasi,* the army, and countless civilians from the town administration, the communist Free German Youth Organization and of course of the Party had all been drawn together to keep the protesting crowd in check, in fact almost outnumbering them. All the streets radiating from the place were blocked by army trucks and water cannons, and men in uniforms formed an almost impenetrable wall. They left gaps for those who wanted to leave the place quietly, of course tearing from them badges and signs thought hostile.

Happily, it didn't get as bad as in other cities like Dresden, Leipzig and Berlin, where the forces of law and order randomly arrested demonstrators, even bystanders and those they thought to be the ringleaders, which was nonsense, there were no ringleaders, and threw them on the trucks. Here the *Greiftrupps* came into play, literally "snatch troops", a kind of riot control squads which were very effective in suddenly charging into a crowd and ripping out people they wanted to get hold of. Before disappearing into the trucks some managed to shout out their names so that friends were able to learn what was happening to them. They were kept in custody for some days, partly maltreated, then processed and sometimes sentenced to prison. Some, the lucky ones, were deported to West Germany. But even in Halle there was such a display of power that we lost all belief in any changes. And we were not the only ones. Timothy Garton Ash in his book "The File" confessed that as late as summer 1989 he wrote in an article for the "Spectator" that he was seeing the immense possibilities of what was happening in Poland and Hungary, but he and his dissident GDR friends did not believe "that change could come so fast in East Germany and that, within a few months people would simply be walking through the Wall".

Then it happened. On the 20th of July (a truly historic date: On 20 July 1944, Claus Graf Schenk von Stauffenberg and other conspirators made their abortive attempt to assassinate Adolf Hitler, Führer of Nazi Germany) we got our first *Laufzettel*, control slip, which, as we had learned from others, was a sure sign that the departure process had irrevocably begun. We were told that we would leave within the third or fourth quarter of the year, but that we should be prepared to leave earlier.

With the *Laufzettel* we had to run to all kinds of administrative places and authorities, even the local water and electricity works to get confirmation that we did not have any outstanding accounts with them. We had to put down the names of all relatives we could think of to make sure we were not indebted to them. We had to draw up lists with every single object we had in our flat: all books with bibliographical data, every knife, fork and spoon, every single piece of furniture, every piece of crockery, kitchen appliances and what not. To the last minute we were harassed by GDR bureaucracy, here used as an instrument for humiliating people.

Of course, we didn't take more than two suitcases and a few bags with us because we were asked to take a certain train to Hanover. This happened on September 8, 1989. We were allowed to arrange with a West German removal company to bring all our things later. Relatives moved into our flat and watched our things.

Sometime around midnight of September 8 we were received by my brother and sister-in-law and friends with open arms and a bottle of champagne. Two months later, on November 9, the Iron Curtain was finally lifted as the Wall came down. I often wonder what would have happened if we had stayed in the GDR. But we didn't regret anything.

11 GREAT EXPECTATIONS

East Germany, communist Germany, the German Democratic Republic, the Soviet Occupation Zone, the Eastern Zone or simply "the Zone"—were there even more names for the country which left its imprint on most of my life? Oh yes. Among ourselves we often called it "the greatest GDR in the world". The then (West German) Federal Chancellor Kurt-Georg Kiesinger—having fully recovered from his exhausting job in the Nazi foreign ministry's radio propaganda department, where he was responsible for that ministry's connection with Goebbels' propaganda ministry—tried to avoid any reference to that country by name and once called it *das Gebilde*, which in the context of the time could be translated as "that strange formation".

And truly, a strange formation it was, one which could be hated and loved at the same time. We used to ask each other the following question—in the presence of members of the communist state party, the *SED*: In future history books, what will the German Democratic Republic be remembered as? Answer: It will be remembered as a cantankerous, tiny little land on the western frontier of China.

But still—what a country it was. Many poor working-class families sent their children to grammar school and university on scholarships. Health services and most pills were free (and prescribed so lavishly that checks near surgeries and pharmacies revealed that people often disposed of the medicine in litter bins). More than ninety per cent of the women went out to work and thus gained unheard of status in the family and in society (up to a certain level). Of course, they had to take their children to the nursery first, sometimes at 5.30 in the morning, and living in the "chemistry triangle" formed by the cities of Halle, Leipzig and Bitterfeld meant joining your peers in the "bronchitis orchestra". Athletes won Olympic medals galore—strange to say, at the expense of physical education at school. People paid ridiculously low rents—and thus most buildings were in bad repair. Bread was so cheap—subsidized by the state—that clever people fed it to their hens and then sold the eggs to the retail trade. They got a higher price—subsidized by the state—for the eggs than it cost to produce them or even to buy them. So, soon they used a short-cut: they bought eggs in one shop and sold them in another for a higher price, pretending that they (the eggs) were the results of their hens' efforts. This was great fun— for some. The majority paid dearly for this kind of economy, and the state was heavily indebted.

Well, life could indeed be great fun. Take cars. You ordered a car. The choice would cause you neither headache nor heartache, since there were only two models to choose from: the Trabant and the Wartburg. Forgive me: there was also the Skoda from Czechoslovakia, if you had the money. And if you had well-to-do relations in West Germany, generally regarded as the class enemy (West Germany, not your relatives), they could give their hard currency to a state-operated organization by the strange name of Genex, which then gave you a car, first of Eastern make, later also of Western.

If you didn't have any such generous friends or relations in the West (and most people didn't), you had to wait for between twelve and fifteen years before it was your turn. Now people were not stupid. As soon as the children turned eighteen, they were entitled to order a car. And, of course, grandparents and relatives who had never thought of buying or even driving a car could order one. As a result, provided you had a little patience, you could have a new car every few years. And, oh wonder, nearly everybody who wanted a car had a car. Another miracle: usually you could sell your used car for at least the amount of money that you needed to buy a new one.

On the spiritual side, there was a great freedom of opinion in my country. You had the freedom to speak your mind as freely and loudly as you wished! Provided that it didn't differ in any way from the opinion of the dominant party, the *SED*. Some fools took their constitutional right of freedom of opinion *literally* instead of *dialectically*, and ended up in Hohenschönhausen, a very safe remand prison of the Ministry of Truth—excuse me, Ministry of State Security—where you could be held for two years without being allowed contact to a lawyer. This helped plenty of people to get back on the path of righteousness. Quite a number shortened their stay by promising to help the Ministry in its endeavors to gather as much information as possible about its charges, *i. e.*, the population of the country.

But here as in many other cases the class enemy in West Germany helped generously. It bought the prisoner, let us say for DM 60,000, and set him or her free in West Germany. So they got their freedom, and the GDR got hard currency, with which it could then buy goods in West Berlin that were urgently needed in Wandlitz, where the members of the Politburo—the high command of the country—lived behind barbed wire and well protected by the comrades of the State Security Police.

As indicated, if you kept mum you could live well. Take your humble author, who kept mum enough to be allowed to study English and German at the Martin-Luther-University in Halle-Wittenberg from 1957 to 1962. No chance of going to England to improve my English, though. Not even after I had made love to a member (female) of the Communist Party of Great Britain who visited the GDR to tell people there about the British Campaign for Nuclear Disarmament and sing the relevant songs (rather shrilly, I have to say). She invited me to London—a dream of cosmic proportions for a student of English in East Germany—on behalf of her London-based Communist Party branch. But the authorities refused to grant me a visa, the reason being that, as the GDR had no diplomatic relations with the UK at that time, they could not let me go unprotected to an imperialist country. So, we had to content ourselves in our institute with a lonely Communist from Liverpool, who had chosen to spend the rest of his life in paradise. But as he was a good teacher and his English was more or less understandable, and as we had an excellent phonetic training, we made do.

To make do, that is what generally helped people to survive and even enjoy life within well-defined limits. For many, East Germany could be an idyll, though in truth a frightful one. The dictatorship appeared in the garb of fatherly love. It rewarded the well-behaved and punished the naughty, not to destroy them, though, but to make them better. If you regretted your outrage you could hope for a mitigation of punishment. The main road to this kind of redemption was self-criticism.

Even those who secretly hated the system and refused to play an active role could find a small corner of peace with like-minded spirits, who often gathered under the protection of the local church. Nationwide the upper echelons of the clergy had made their peace with the regime. A sizable number served the secret police as informants. But parish priests opened their churches on Mondays for all who wanted to take part in what came to be called "peace prayers". The secret police sent their people to these prayers to learn who had taken part and what had been said. Your author once heard the minister of a church in the city of Halle greet those present with the words "I am particularly glad to welcome those among you who came here not so much to pray but to listen and to observe. Let us include them and their families in our prayers." With this he looked at some people sitting at the back for so long that everybody turned their heads to look at them, too. And, hard as it may be to believe, some of them even blushed.

But most people in East Germany had made a kind of deal with the regime, persuading themselves that they didn't really participate in the prevailing injustice but only pretended to. They were able to develop a very efficient doublethink. At work they talked the way official propaganda demanded, but privately they longed for the sort of life that was shown on West German television.

Understandably, this difficult tight-rope walk didn't leave people undamaged. Drinking was widespread, and the GDR belonged to the countries with the highest per capita consumption of alcohol. People sought to compensate for their frustration by seeking as many sexual encounters as possible, men and women alike. And if this was not possible for some, they at least told each other dirty and, even more often, political jokes. The rate of suicide was high and so was the rate of mental illness.

Does all this sound contradictory, inconsistent? If so, it sounds right, because the system *was* contradictory, inconsistent and, to a high degree, openly ridiculous. But it was dangerous, even lethal, for those who decided that they had to resist, to dissent, to speak up.

That was a glimpse of the background against which my family and I applied for emigration to West Germany. It was only after my wife had lost her job and after repeated interrogations by the secret police that we were finally granted permission to leave the country.

We crossed the frontier six weeks before the Berlin Wall came down, after which you could travel freely. Still, we were happy enough not to feel ridiculous.

Hanover in Lower Saxony was where my brother lived. He had left East Germany in 1953, at the tender age of fifteen, at a time when the frontier between East and West Berlin was still open. You simply got on the municipal railway and went west. He put us up, and we had the chance of unhurriedly getting used to life in the free world.

I was fifty years old when we left East Germany and came to the west.

Suddenly, money-procuring eggs, cars, mental illness, casual sexual encounters, and so on all lost their importance and other things came to the foreground. The gift of doublethink that I mentioned above was now applied to the contradictions of a *democratic* society, which was less harmful to one's health.

As we had always watched West German television and talked to our relatives who had come to visit us in East Germany, there were many things that did not surprise us, but others did.

In the allegedly money-determined, materialistically-minded cold capitalist world we met mainly friendly people—and that says a lot, seeing that we were in Lower Saxony. Even the police, the local authorities, people in the labor exchange, the housing office and the town hall were helpful.

The first shock I had was when I tried to buy some meat, or was it sausage, for the family. The display of meat products in the supermarket appeared to me so large, the choice so exaggerated, even superfluous, almost sinful, that I had to break off my shopping and hurry home because I feared I was going to be sick. While I got used to many other things fairly quickly, it took me longest to come to terms with the extravagance, the squandering, with respect to food.

I was lucky enough to get a job at a small university near Hanover very soon as a lecturer in English. Though I was just filling in for a colleague who had gone to America on paternity leave for two years, I struck a bonanza. Firstly, because I earned what I regarded at that time as a lot of money, and secondly, because I underwent a kind of forced socialization in a very short time, which would otherwise (probably) have taken many years.

There is a myth concerning the differing work ethics in East and West Germany before the reunification of the country. The West Germans generally believed that the East Germans were a lazy lot who after 1989 had to be taught what it was like to work hard. Now, at my new place of work I was surprised to find that the work load you took upon yourself was defined by you yourself. If you wanted to take it easy, workwise, you could. Nobody cared, except maybe the students. But since they had to pass examinations and therefore didn't want to alienate their examiners, *i. e.*, their lecturers, they rarely complained.

In a comparable position in East Germany I had had to teach twenty forty-five-minute periods a week and spend at least another twenty hours doing administration and research. In my new academic institution, it was twelve hours teaching and not much else (if you so decided). Some members of staff, some of them quite senior, managed to come to work only two and a half days per week. The rest could be whiled away at home, with some people earning money on the side by doing translations or writing reports for industrial enterprises. To be fair, though, the majority of the staff worked their share, some of them even more than that, and so helped to keep the university going.

What topped it all was what I later learned during a summer term spent at another German university. The paternity leave colleague had come back from America and I had to find a new job. I had heard on the grapevine that at the University of X somebody in the field of English teacher training wanted to take a year's sabbatical and so they needed a temporary lecturer. As I had never before worked in this area, training future English teachers, my expertise was—to say the least—rudimentary. But to my lasting amazement both the students and I myself survived. This must have had something to do with that peculiarity of work in academia, where you so often disguise your lack of knowledge by euphonious and often mysterious words or word-combinations that are difficult to understand and therefore difficult to contradict.

In my academic life in the east this had not been so, probably because Marxist-Leninist vocabulary was expected to be stringent, unambiguous, and not in the least fanciful.

But this was not the surprising new discovery that I referred to earlier. This stupendous item was the piece of advice that I got from a well-meaning comrade-in-arms when I arranged my timetable for the term. Why didn't I put four hours of class (of my weekly twelve) on Friday afternoon, he queried, eyebrows raised? I said that in my experience students didn't appreciate seminars on Friday afternoons and thus the classes might have to be cancelled. He looked me straight in the eye for quite some time, until I—clumsy beast from the East—understood. No further word was required, and my working week for that term thereafter consisted of eight teaching periods a week. Henceforth I called this the "Friday method".

That same colleague had organized his own timetable in an enviably ingenious way, which showed the creativity that is possible in a capitalist free-enterprise society as compared to the unproductive and inefficient command society I had escaped from. The colleague, who as a senior lecturer had to teach only eight hours of seminars a week, had managed to put all his teaching on one day, Monday, after reducing it by means of the Friday method to six hours. The rest of the time he spent in his privately-run esoteric marriage counseling office just opposite the main building of the university. This helped him to put aside a nice little bundle, which he needed, however, as he had been divorced a few times and had to take financial care of his former wives and his children. Also, through his marriage counseling he had found himself a girlfriend—and she happened to be someone who was not to be enjoyed cheaply.

After the term was over, I went back to my small university in Lower Saxony, where in the meantime a professorship in English language teaching had been put on the market. Now it is often so in Germany that it takes years to find a suitable professor. And it did. So happy me could fill in for four years.

Sometime afterwards, I had a recurring dream that gave me the fright of my life: Communist hardliners in the Soviet Union had won their coup d'état against President Mikhail Gorbachev. The hardliners had led the crumbling Soviet

Union back into the Ice Age of Stalinist Communism. Newly united Germany was to be split up again and East Germany to be returned to the Soviet Union. All former East Germans now living in the West were to be repatriated (if need be by force) to East Germany. The police (West German) came to our house and marched my family and me to the station in Hanover where the train to East Berlin was waiting.

Just as we were on the point of being bundled onto the train, I woke up, my heart beating wildly. I realized where I was, calmed down and felt in a moment of unbelievable happiness that, after all, my great expectations had been fulfilled.

12 GDR Revisited

After the Wall's dramatic fall on 9 November 1989 I was eager to return to the country of my youth, happiness and grief. I went as often as my new job at a West German university allowed, and always I found the country and the people changed.

The first time was at the end of November 1989. When I approached the checkpoint at Helmstedt/Marienborn on the autobahn between Hanover (in the West) and Magdeburg (in the East) I felt like the poet Heinrich Heine must have felt when he, coming from Paris, arrived at the German border:

> *It was in the dreary month of November,*
> *The gloomy days grew shorter,*
> *The wind tore the foliage from the trees,*
> *As I approached the German border.*
> *And as I reached the border line,*
> *I felt a mightier throb*
> *Within my chest, I even think,*
> *I nearly began to sob.*

The former checkpoint with its formidable installations was almost abandoned, and I was waved through by a border guard, who just 6 weeks before would have shot at me had I tried to drive through without permission, albeit from East to West. The checkpoint had been manned with as many as 1,000 passport control, customs and border police officials.

The buildings had been linked by an underground tunnel system through which military or police units could reach the control portal quickly and secretly. Checkpoint was the name given it by the Western side, the GDR called it *Grenz-übergangsstelle* (which literally means "border-crossing-place"). I had the strangest emotions when I drove through the gate and on to the "German Democratic Republic, the first Workers' and Peasants' State on German soil".

What had happened that brought about the downfall of the communist regime? Where had all the power gone, which until only a few weeks ago had dominated the greater part of my life, had secretly watched all my movements, had kept me confined within its borders, forbidden me to read certain newspapers, had allowed no criticism of the government in public, had threatened me with prison should I dare produce anti-government literature, had controlled my telephone calls, sacked my wife from her job because of our exit permit application, prohibited me from traveling to England or other lands of my desire?

This power had looked so formidable that up to the very end people had feared what was termed the "Chinese solution". That referred to the violent suppression of political protests on Beijing's Tiananmen Square in June 1989, where hundreds were killed and over a thousand imprisoned. The *SED* had called the events in China "counterrevolutionary" and their suppression a victory over the counter-revolutionaries, so it could be anticipated how the *SED* was planning to deal with potential protests in the GDR. And really, it needed some effort from a number of Politburo members to restrain Secretary-General Erich Honecker from ordering an army tank regiment to drive through Leipzig and crush the mounting Monday protest marches. For those who had planned to dethrone Erich Honecker the renouncement of violence had been the imperative condition for their palace revolution. Any escalation of violence would have made the possibility of a peaceful transition impossible and destroyed all hopes of the self-styled reformers coming to power. And most important, since Gorbachev had let it be known that the Soviet Union would no longer intervene in its socialist satellite countries by military force, the GDR regime was left to its own devices, which looked so formidable but were in fact only effective if they were, for example, willing to open fire on 70,000 demonstrators in Leipzig on 9 October. The rulers were divided among themselves about what course to take, and the people had started to lose their fear. What is more, the protesters' commitment to non-violent resistance, expressed on their banners and symbolized by their carrying candles, disarmed the military, particularly the "Combat Groups of the Working Class", parts of which flatly refused to follow orders in Leipzig to use force against the demonstrators. One of *Stasi* minister Mielke's underlings was heard to say: You can't fight against candles in front of church entrances.

But still, a "Chinese solution" was not out of the question, depending on who would win the power struggle in the Politburo.

Erich Honecker, who was also Chairman of the National Defense Council of the German Democratic Republic and thus supreme military commander had at his disposal

— a secret police employing 91,000 staff and having the help of about 200,000 informers, which taking into regard the size of the population (in the end roughly 16.6 million) was the largest secret police apparatus in the history of mankind,

— an army that NATO officers rated the best in the Warsaw Pact, the Soviet Army included, although it numbered only 120,000 men, this reputation being based on discipline, thoroughness of training, and the quality of the officer leadership,

— the paramilitary Combat Groups of the Working Class, essentially a Party army, totaling approximately 210,000 "fighters" (*Kämpfer*),

— a police force (People's Police—*Volkspolizei*) numbering about 80,000 full-time police officers and 177,500 volunteers,

— 262 sectional party leadership teams *(SED Kreis-leitungen)* equipped with firearms, as of course were all full-time *SED* functionaries from that level upward,

— a backup in the shape of Soviet troops, which were the largest contingent of soldiers in history kept abroad by an occupation power for such a period of time, 45 years: in 1991 before the great withdrawal began, 338,000 troops, 4200 tanks, 8200 armored vehicles, 3600 guns, 690 aircraft, 680 helicopters, 180 rocket systems, more than a

100.000 motor vehicles, 677.000 tons of ammunition as well as numerous additional military equipment. But of course, Honecker must have divined that those forces would no longer be ready to fight uprisings in the GDR, as they had in June 1953. But nobody could be absolutely sure, as the later putsch against Gorbachev in August 1991 indicated.

The question of "where had all the power gone" occurred to me every time I crossed the border, which was at first still physically in existence, and never left me until I settled down in Weimar in what is now simply the eastern part of Germany. It gave me the idea to write down some aspects of life, my own individual memories and experiences, in the former GDR, the *ehemalige DDR*, as it is commonly called today. This I did in the belief that some answers could be found in the ridiculously huge gap between the ideology of official politics and reality of the living experience.

The reader can make up their own mind about what is true or not. Different persons remember differently, and the more distant the past becomes, the more blurred the images get, the more urgent it is to record what it was like. My grandchildren as well as friends from America and England continue asking me about the GDR and want to know what life was like. This they do in view of the glorification of the past by socialist hardliners or people who hold to the belief "that not everything was bad in the GDR" (by which people in truth mean most of the things were good) and a kind of demonization quite common in some media and under-standably promoted by those who really suffered under the regime.

I chose English for my memories because it helped put a greater distance between me and the events which shaped my life and my way of thinking for the long period from 1949 to 1989, the forty years the GDR existed. This distance I believe makes me see things more clearly and more impartially, in a way as if using the eyes of a foreigner. I would also like to create some understanding for the people in East Germany, the great majority of whom had made their peace with the regime, because, if they kept quiet and showed at least a minimum affirmative attitude, they enjoyed a better (material) living standard, safer jobs, larger security in daily life, better education for their children, better and cheaper housing, better health service than most people in the world, and certainly much better than their socialist brothers and sisters in the much praised Soviet Union, the fatherland of all working people. The last point was of course never admitted openly, but lots of GDR folks knew it, particularly those who worked for a time in the Soviet Union or visited it.

All this made people overlook the decaying inner cities, the lack of environmental protection, the waste of energy, the constant smell of lignite used for heating and the slow but inevitable death of a communist command society. Often, to me personally, things appeared to be on an upward trend. For example, my daughters after having finished high school, were able to go on and study medicine, not, I admit, without the help of an uncle who knew the Deputy Minister of Higher Education, but still, they were on their way.

We moved from smaller apartments to bigger ones, had a car and a garden with a small dacha, got on in our jobs and so, living in one of the new socialist cities, tended to be blind to the general decay of the country. This we had in common with most people in the GDR who without having an alternative adjusted their lives and found something like identification, not with the regime, but with the circumstances of their existence, with the adversities they mastered, with their own individual achievements despite limited options, and even with a special kind of solidarity, though it grew out of a shared feeling of dissatisfaction.

Humans are born with the will to survive, the ability to endure injustices, abide by rules that defy basic common sense as long as they are let live. Only very few are born to be brave protesters and even resistance fighters who would rather go to prison than live a life imposed on them against their will. To the majority, the possibility of a small interruption in their careers, the danger of their children not getting the high school or university education they desire, the most marginal risk to their living standards makes them think twice before doing anything that might create problems.

I myself am a good example of the majority mentioned. During my adult life, say from 1960 to 1986, when I applied for an exit permit to West Germany, I grumbled, cracked political jokes and tried whenever I was able to insert some common sense into the progress reports I had to write about our work in the English department to the university administration, always knowing how far I could venture and stopping short before saying anything that could be rated as too critical or even subversive. I cleverly handled what was later called inner censorship or the scissors in one's head, that is the ability to know what was ideologically and politically desired and what was not, a variety of Orwellian doublethink. So I made my tiny career from simple lecturer to deputy head of the Foreign Language Department at Merseburg University, and only in 1986, at the age of forty-seven, when my dissatisfaction with the political circumstances, my desire to live a self-determined life and above all to travel to England, my spiritual second home, became so over-whelming did I apply for permission to leave.

When on my first trip back in November 1989 I approached my birthplace and longtime home city of Halle on the Saale river, I was stopped by a big straw fire in the middle of the highway. Farmers or farm workers stood around, feeding the fire with ever new straw bales, torn apart. A traffic policeman stood helplessly to the side and advised me not to say anything to the farmers as they were enraged and aggressive and they wouldn't be happy to see my West German license plate. I turned around and parked my car at some distance from the fire. Then I went to one of the bystanders, said I was from Halle and asked what had made them so angry. He replied hadn't I heard that the West German farmers' association was lobbying the government to dissolve the huge GDR agricultural cooperatives in favor of the old small individual farm enterprises that were preferred by the Federal (West German) agricultural policy, and they would lose their jobs because the old farmers would demand their lands back and others would come from West Germany and buy the land.

The friendly policeman, still in his old *Volkspolizei* (People's Police) uniform, told me how to get to Halle by a detour over dirt roads.

My first destination was Halle-Neustadt, the socialist city, my longtime place of residence, and where on that day I could barely trust my eyes. All order seemed to have disappeared. People parked their cars—lots of them West German make—on the green patches ignoring the parking spaces (of which there were plenty), and the damage done to the turf and plants which some had so lovingly cared for. It was as if after long years of being disciplined by an almighty state they needed to show their defiance of everything that smelled of authority, even if it meant damaging their own personal environment. There was litter everywhere, the little parks were unkempt, the entrances to the big apartment blocks upswept and panes in some doors were broken, sights previously unheard of. One lonely policeman tried to convince a resident to park his car in a parking space, but the man simply said: "You can't order me about any more." And the policeman went quietly away.

I went to our old block to visit a friend or rather an acquaintance who had been chairwoman of the Halle-Neustadt Democratic Women's League of Germany, an organization controlled by the communist party, the *SED*. During GDR times she had repeatedly gotten into trouble with the Party district organization at Halle because instead of bringing the Halle-Neustadt Women's League in line with Party politics, she helped them with the problems of their daily lives, encouraged them to stand up to their husbands, invited doctors to instruct them in questions of health care and education and similar issues. But because she had the backing of a woman in the presidium of the Free German Trade Union Federation, who was also a member of the *SED* Central Committee, she got away with this liberal interpretation of her political duties. The woman whose support she'd had, committed suicide in January 1990 because of allegations of corruption, never to be proven.

My acquaintance let me in and told me about the hard time she was having. People accused her of having been an informant of the *Stasi* (for which there was no proof), of having used her position in the Women's League for her own advantage and similar offenses. But I had known her in my time in Halle-Neustadt and could have vouched for her honesty. As she had been a fulltime political functionary, she had of course now lost her job and income and didn't know what would become of her. I later learned that she was granted a small pension by the state and was able to live quietly.

The old city of Halle, to which I drove then, looked no more encouraging than Halle-Neustadt, even though the shop windows were already displaying Western goods—often cheap and flimsy but which people were eagerly buying. There were remnants of GDR products still to be seen, but they for the most part were now unwanted, though some of them good quality. Of course, all things from the West had to be better.

I stopped in front of a building which had housed, or was still housing, a part of the town administration called *Abteilung Inneres*, Department for Home Affairs, which, after three long years of waiting, had granted my exit visa from the GDR. I wanted to see whether the old occupants of the offices were still there, and possibly speak to them. It was a foolish idea, because they would certainly not have wanted to talk about their role in keeping people confined and in uncertainty about their future. But there was nobody there, a note pinned to the door told visitors to go to the town hall, where their concerns would presumably be addressed.

After a while, I decided to go back to my current home in Hanover. I was depressed and sad but didn't know why. What had I expected? The country was in transition, one state had disappeared, the other had not yet arrived. What cheered me up a bit was the apparent absence of people wanting to take their revenge, who wanted to physically punish those who had, in effect, taken part of their lives away. Or had they? Perhaps people's own tacit complicity, the choice of a relative security, personal freedom or not, had persuaded them to keep silent and live as well as possible within the system in which they found themselves. And simply wait for the future.

Some of those who had seriously suffered tried to bring their informers or even Stasi tormenters to trial, but mostly without success. It was difficult to prove that they had been beaten or otherwise maltreated. A number got (or are still getting) compensation from the government for the time they had spent in prison or for the damage caused by being fired from their jobs. One of my brothers told me that he had met a former acquaintance who had informed on him, but that man had said to him, you must understand, they threatened me, what should I have done? So, my brother had just let it go. I didn't hear or read of a case where somebody had physically harmed one of those people. Very few, maybe a handful, of *Stasi* officers committed suicide, and also some informers.

A particularly tragic fate was that of Barbara Neuhoff (name changed), a teacher from Weimar. In 1971, when still a teacher trainee, she was recruited by a friend, a neighbor, to work for the Ministry of State Security, *Stasi*, as an informant. She met several times with *Stasi* officers in a safe house and received, at least once, a reward of 50 GDR marks (which would have bought her four packages of ground coffee). Some months later, in June 1971, this cooperation ended. According to her *Stasi* file her case officer reported to his superiors that her information was of no "operative value". Which means in plain words she didn't tell anything of interest. In the following decades Barbara Neuhoff specialized in teaching disabled children, a work not highly regarded in the GDR. Parents remember how dedicated she was in that difficult and demanding job. After 1989 she became a civil servant in the new land of Thuringia, working as a consultant for special needs schools. In the summer of 1991 she was asked to fill in a questionnaire, on which the first question was: Did you cooperate with the Ministry for State Security? Yes or no. Barbara felt trapped: If she answered yes, she would lose her job, as she would if she lied and was found out. She answered no and henceforth lived in fear that her file would be found. Out of utter shame she didn't dare confide to anybody, not even her husband or her best friend, who both noted that she was changed, depressed. Obviously, her file was found because she was asked to appear before the committee in Erfurt that had to decide what to do with her. They told her that her chances of keeping her job were poor but that the decision was left to the Minister of Education, who had the final say in such difficult cases. She would hear from them. Barbara didn't return home to Weimar. She booked a hotel room, where she was found by the chambermaid the next morning, lifeless, an empty bottle of cognac and empty boxes of painkillers and tranquillizers on the bedside table. So, the Minister was spared a decision.

The case officer, who lived to see reunified Germany, was never brought to trial, because he had worked according to the laws of the GDR. He got his pension as a civil servant from the government, though somewhat reduced, against which he protested with other comrades, futilely. That led them to call the new state undemocratic and prone to victor's justice. People like Barbara mustn't be forgotten, and their utter misery and fear should be taken into account when there is talk about the former socialist state and how it treated its people.

My next trip to East Germany was in the summer of 1990. In the first free balloting in March 1990 the *SED,* now renamed the Party of Democratic Socialism, had suffered a crushing defeat. The eastern counterpart of West German Chancellor Helmut Kohl's Christian Democrats, which had pledged a speedy reunification of Germany, emerged as the largest political party in East Germany's first democratically elected People's Chamber. A new East German government headed by Lothar de Maizière, a long-time member of the eastern Christian Democratic Union, and backed initially by a broad coalition of other parties, began negotiations for a treaty of unification. A tide of refugees to West Germany that threatened to cripple the East Germany economy added urgency to those negotiations. In July that crisis was somewhat eased by a monetary union of the two Germanys that gave East Germans the long-desired deutschmark, the hard currency of the Federal Republic.

In contrast to my first visit the atmosphere was now one of seemingly unlimited enthusiasm. The *Stasi* had been dissolved, and there was a sense of enjoyment, a feeling that everything was possible. A kind of positive anarchy ruled, which allowed people to overlook the growing number of compatriots out of jobs because factories had been closed down.

I drove to Berlin to pay a visit to the Death Strip, the infamous Wall, which had already partly been pulled down. Some East Berliners had decided to make this death strip a sea of flowers by sowing lupines on it, and they had even convinced former border guards to help with an old army truck.

It was an interim period, in which people didn't need official approvals for doing things, didn't ask authorities for permits, and everybody had the chance of doing what they had always wanted and going where they had always wanted.

Of course, there was a dark side to the new freedom. On the streets people enjoyed a kind of jester's license, parked wildly, raced through red traffic lights, hit and ran, and the uncertain and conflicted police in their obsolete cars weren't able to stop them, if they even tried. Bank robbers equipped with fast Western cars had a high time for a while. Legal proceedings had to be postponed because witnesses didn't show up at court, having no fear of consequences. Law enforcement of the old system, accustomed to receiving and following orders, had no effective leadership and no idea how to regain their lost authority. Rip-off artists, fraudsters and adventurers (many from the West) took advantage of this new anarchy, black markets were in full blossom and cigarette smugglers raked in phenomenally.

But relief and contentment with this new life were predominant. In Weimar, I saw how young people had occupied an abandoned house and without having asked anybody for permission, founded a *Kulturcafé*. Bands performed, ignored closing time, nobody came to check. It was, one young man told me, a liberation for his generation.

Liberation it was, but not liked by some. Street vendors sold dildos, pornographic journals and sex toys, things that most East Germans only knew by hearsay. Nobody thought about the laws protecting youth, and the legal vacuum was exploited widely.

People who had been following orders for 40 years now suddenly scorned regulation. Liquor licenses, business licenses, food control, book keeping and taxes – nobody cared.

The new order left its imprint. Soldiers in the army elected soldiers' councils, employees of the state-controlled radio, tv and newspapers made their voices heard in the editorial meetings, prisoners revolted, formed prisoners' councils and went on hunger strikes to force the prison authorities to implement a more humane regime.

Some folks in Leipzig founded their own television station, because after 40 years of controlled media they wanted to broadcast their own news. Their "Channel X" transmitted until it was closed down after the reunification in October 1990. The Federal Post Office, then the state broadcasting authority, forbid its continued operation, and as in all the other areas, law and order slowly but inevitably crept back. But the feeling that remained, even thirty years later, was expressed by a now no longer young man: It was a fantastic, wild and vibrant time. It might have done the reunified Germany good had it lasted a bit longer, given the unavoidable bureaucratic complications of modern German life.

When I came back from my last trip before reunification on October 3, 1990, I had a feeling of *zufriedenheit,* satisfaction. One of the great empires of the world, and along with it the government of East Germany, had fallen apart – in a very short span of three years – without violence and suppression, peacefully.

The final barrier to reunification was overcome in July 1990 when Federal Chancellor Kohl prevailed upon Gorbachev to drop his objections to a unified Germany within the NATO alliance in return for sizable (West) German financial aid to the Soviet Union. A unification treaty was ratified by the *Bundestag* (West German Parliament) and the

Volkskammer (East German Parliament) in September and went into effect on October 3, 1990. The German Democratic Republic joined the Federal Republic as five additional *Länder*, states, and the two parts of divided Berlin became one *Land*. The five new *Länder* were Brandenburg, Mecklenburg-West Pomerania, Saxony, Saxony-Anhalt, and Thuringia.

The latter has become my true and genuine *Heimat*.

ABOUT THE AUTHOR

Christoph Werner was born in the East German city of Halle on the Saale river and raised as the son of a Lutheran minister. He studied English and German at Martin Luther University at Halle and worked at various universities in East and West Germany before retiring to live in Weimar.

He has written four novels, biographical sketches and numerous short stories and essays.

ALSO BY CHRISTOPH WERNER

SHADOWS OF MY FATHER
THE MEMOIRS OF MARTIN LUTHER'S SON
A Novel
Translated by Michael Leonard

An enthralling and original novel that brings to life one of Christianity's most significant figures, Martin Luther, and the tumultuous world of late medieval Germany that shaped him—and was reshaped by him—told by his youngest son, Paul.

Unwilling to join his father's fanatical disciples, Paul became critical of his famous father's critiques and instead turned his interest and intellect to science and medicine. Yet Martin Luther remained a presence that haunted Paul's life and transformed his world.

Shadows of My Father paints a vivid and atmospheric picture of Martin Luther, including his day-to-day life, his break with the Catholic Church, and his singular dedication in sustaining the Reformation. It is also a portrait of a son raised in a harsh religious household who turns his faith to saving lives instead of souls, eventually becoming a royal doctor.

Christoph Werner vividly re-creates the world of sixteenth-century Germany, a time of wars and famines when a Kaiser battles to keep an empire together and when faith and tradition clash with education and reason—giving birth to superstition and shaking the foundations of a Catholic Church already riven by internal conflict. A thoughtful, insightful lens into one of the most famous figures, one of the most profound historical events, and one of the most turbulent periods in our past, *Shadows of My Father* reveals an intriguing, historically accurate, and all-too-human side of Martin Luther and his lasting legacy.

Harper Legend 2017, ISBN: 978-0062846525 (Paperback)
eBook available

TO LIVE IN ALL ETERNITY
Caspar David Friedrich and
Joseph Mallord William Turner

A Novel
Edited by Michael Leonard

Caspar David Friedrich's dark, melancholic view of life and Joseph Mallard William Turner's full-blooded engagement with the world around him characterize this novel. Despite the contrast between them, these two romantic painters are connected by the uniqueness of their art.

Friedrich's works became part of an existential awareness of life. Turner, with his powerful use of light and color, paved the way for a new impressionistic art form.

The novel lets the reader experience an encounter of intimate distance between the two painters and opens the world of their images, their motives and their times.

Tredition 2019. ISBN 978-3-7497-1975-4 (Paperback)
eBook available

BOOKS BY CHRISTOPH WERNER

Der Bronstein-Defekt und andere Geschichten

Schloss am Strom. Die Geschichte vom Leben und Sterben des Baumeisters Karl Friedrich Schinkel

Um ewig einst zu leben. Caspar David Friedrich und Joseph Mallord William Turner. Roman

To Live in all Eternity. Caspar David Friedrich and Joseph Mallord William Turner. A Novel.

Buckingham Palace. Roman

Wintermorgen— Geschichten und Geschichtliches

Paulus Luther. Sein Leben von ihm selbst aufgeschrieben. Wahrhaftiger Roman

Shadows of My Father. The Memoirs of Martin Luther's Son. A Novel

Mitgelaufen. (Geschichten aus einem untergegangenen Land)

Lifting the Iron Curtain. Tales from a Bygone Country

Zeitfracht Medien GmbH
Ferdinand-Jühlke-Straße 7
99095 Erfurt, Deutschland
produktsicherheit@kolibri360.de